RIPPLE

RIPPLE

MANDY HUBBARD

razOr
bill

An Imprint of Penguin Group (USA) Inc.

Ripple

RAZORBILL

Published by the Penguin Group
Penguin Young Readers Group
345 Hudson Street, New York, New York 10014, U.S.A.
Penguin Group (USA) Inc., 375 Hudson Street, New York, New York 10014, U.S.A.
Penguin Group (Canada), 90 Eglinton Avenue East, Suite 700, Toronto, Ontario, Canada
M4P 2Y3 (a division of Pearson Penguin Canada Inc.)
Penguin Books Ltd, 80 Strand, London WC2R 0RL, England
Penguin Ireland, 25 St Stephen's Green, Dublin 2, Ireland (a division of Penguin Books Ltd)
Penguin Group (Australia), 250 Camberwell Road, Camberwell, Victoria 3124, Australia
(a division of Pearson Australia Group Pty Ltd)
Penguin Books India Pvt Ltd, 11 Community Centre, Panchsheel Park,
New Delhi – 110 017, India
Penguin Group (NZ), 67 Apollo Drive, Mairangi Bay, Auckland 1311, New Zealand
(a division of Pearson New Zealand Ltd)
Penguin Books (South Africa) (Pty) Ltd, 24 Sturdee Avenue, Rosebank, Johannesburg
2196, South Africa

Penguin Books Ltd, Registered Offices: 80 Strand, London WC2R 0RL, England

10 9 8 7 6 5 4 3 2 1

ISBN 978-1-59514-423-2

Library of Congress Cataloging-in-Publication Data is available

Printed in the United States of America

For Rachel, a best friend in every sense of the word.

CHAPTER ONE

The first boy I ever loved, Steven Goode, was really into cars. He received a junky '72 Chevelle for his sixteenth birthday and spent six months rebuilding it. Everyone in school knew about it because Steven worked on it during shop class, and half the guys at Cedar Cove High helped him, wrenching and sanding and polishing until every piece was as good as new.

After it was complete, Steven cruised up and down the streets near the boardwalk, one arm hanging out the window, that adorable lopsided grin never leaving his face.

Then I killed him. I drowned him in the ocean just a few hundred yards from my own sweet-sixteen party.

I don't swim in the ocean anymore. After Steven, I began driving up into the mountains. I found a small, isolated lake, all but hidden by the dense forest. It's glacier-fed and cold as ice, but I swim in it every night anyway, emerging with blue lips and stiff joints.

It's who I am. After that birthday . . . everything changed. I don't sleep anymore; I simply swim, night after night after night. Up here, no one dies. For two years, I haven't killed.

But tonight, I stand in the shadows behind a tree, watching as Cole Hitchings skips rocks across the surface of the lake. Of *my* lake.

I suppose it's poetic justice that it would be Steven's best friend to take this from me, to rob me of the one thing I want most, but I'm not amused. It took weeks to find this place, this perfect, secluded paradise, and Cole is standing over there as if it's his.

My nails dig into the bark of the big cedar as I stare, my eyes narrowed in anger. Frustration boils through my veins, building, growing, coiling in my stomach, so intense I want to scream at him. He shouldn't be here. He doesn't know how much I need the water, how dangerous it is to be standing between me and the lake. Oblivious, he's simply tossing rocks, watching them skip once, twice, three times along the glassy surface. The woods are silent, nothing but quiet shadows—except for the plink, plink, plunk sound of the rocks as they skip. The moon glows across the water, shimmery, yellow.

Miles of jagged foothills and evergreen forest separate the two of us from the rest of the world.

Cole has thick, unruly dark hair and even darker eyes—I can't see them in the moonlight. He's wearing chinos or slacks or something and a light button-down—pale yellow, as far as I can tell, but I'm not sure in the darkness. He's always been the overdressed one at school. Like it's the Ivy League and not a public high school in a tiny coastal town.

He throws rocks like a seasoned pro, though I know he's not an *athlete,* at least not in the normal sense of the word. He was never enough of a team player to handle organized sports. Unless you count skirt-chasing, in which case he could be an Olympic medalist.

His muscles bunch and stretch beneath his shirt as he effortlessly flicks one rock after another into the water. When he runs out of rocks, he leans over and scoops up another handful, tossing them one at a time. He moves with a confident, graceful ease, a little like me under the water. Like a guy who is comfortable in his own skin.

My grip on the tree tightens and splinters dig in, wedging beneath my nails. I inhale sharply at the bite of pain, but I don't take my eyes off Cole. My anger boils as seconds tick past. If I don't swim tonight, I will pay for it tomorrow. My stomach will twist and turn until it feels as if it's in a thousand knots, and I won't be able to eat. My legs will cramp and threaten to buckle underneath me. My forehead will feel hot to the touch.

But if I swim . . . if I give in . . . Cole will join his once best friend, six feet under at Seaside Cemetery.

Why is he here? This lake is in the center of Tillamook State Forest, which spans over three hundred thousand acres. Surely, there is somewhere else in this place he could go.

I lean into the tree, resting my forehead against the rough bark, closing my eyes and inhaling the cedar scent as I will him to leave. Despite the cool September night, I feel feverish. Just being near the water makes me ache for it, makes my skin tingle with the desire to run until I am chest-deep and the water wraps around my skin like a satin ribbon, making the worries, the aches, the stress unwind.

Sometimes, I wonder if this is how a recovering alcoholic would feel if someone put a beer in her hand. If her body would wage war against her mind as mine does.

With every second that passes, I am closer to giving in, and I hate myself for that. He's only a couple dozen yards away, close enough that I could be right in front of him before he'd have a chance to react. I consider marching over to him, screaming at him, telling him that the lake belongs to me. Would he leave? Or would it make things worse? Maybe it would tick him off, and he'd come back every night just to get under my skin.

I purse my eyes tighter, my thick lashes brushing my cheeks. I know exactly how far I am from the water, exactly how many steps it would take for me to dip my toes in the cool, refreshing surface.

The only thing between me and relief is Cole.

I grit my teeth and turn away from the lake. I can make it one night. But if he's here tomorrow, I don't know if I'll be able to resist.

I don't know if he'll live.

CHAPTER TWO

As if the first day of senior year isn't bad enough, I'm physically ill from not swimming, and it's far worse than I remember. Each step I take feels as if shards of glass wedge further into my skin. It's hard to keep up a mask of composure when all I want to do is wince, gasp out in pain, curl into a ball.

Someone rams into my right shoulder, and I careen into the wall, bouncing off the white-painted cinder block hard enough to knock the wind from my lungs. They scream for oxygen, and I nearly bend over and gasp for air, but instead I just blink back the stars and glance over at my tormenter.

It's Nikki. A girl from my old clique. Her deep green eyes are cold and angry, so different from freshman year, when we were bio partners. When we joked around and worked straight through lunch, getting perfect grades on every lab report. Just like the others, she doesn't understand why I shut her out. She never will, because I'll never tell her the truth.

She looks beautiful, in a cream-colored sweater and a string of pink pearls. I feel a stab to the chest. We used to shop for our back-to-school clothes *together.*

"*Frigid.*"

I hear the word, whispered, but purposely loud and close enough for me to overhear. I spin around, but I'm not sure who said it. I tighten my grip on my backpack straps, raking in a deep breath to calm the burning in my lungs. I try to picture myself as I will be tonight, when I slip into the lake and serenity replaces the tension in my back. I must envision the lake thirty, forty times on a normal day, and something tells me today will be much worse.

I purse my lips and try to forget Nikki and the whispers and head down the hall again, past the bulletin board for the school-club signup sheets, past a poster advertising auditions for the fall play, past the trophy cases. Those things meant something to me once, but now I rush past them as if I'm wearing blinders, pretending I don't ache for the things I force myself to forget.

I feel the stares as I pass a group of senior guys sitting near the windows. Their longing gazes eat at me as much as the looks of contempt I get from my former friends. One of them clearly has a girlfriend because she smacks him and then turns to glare at me.

"It's not my fault they stare," I try to tell her with my eyes. I'm wearing the most nondescript clothes in my closet: a pair of jeans and a long-sleeve black V-neck, a scuffed pair of ballet flats on my feet. My hair, long and straight, is pulled back in a low ponytail. I'm not wearing makeup, but I know it doesn't matter—my skin is flawless, my lashes dark and thick even without mascara.

I walk as briskly as possible, until I'm three doors down and can take my seat in English class. As the weight comes off my feet, I clamp my jaw down so that I don't actually sigh aloud. It's never hurt this badly before. I don't know what that means. It's been months since I last skipped swimming. That was when my last lake was overrun by campers, and I had to move.

The new lake was working, until Cole showed up. How did he find it? Why was he there?

I don't know if I have the energy . . . the willpower to start the process all over and find a new lake. I hope he doesn't go back.

I'm resting my head on my desk, my eyes shut, when I hear the chair beside me creak with the weight of another student. It must be the last available chair or no one would sit in it.

"Lexi, you don't look so good," he says.

My mouth goes dry. *Please don't let it be Cole.*

I turn to scowl at him, but when our eyes meet, all I can do is stare, my breath caught in my throat. His eyes are a startling bright shade of hazel. How have I never noticed that? How have I always thought they were a simple dull shade of brown?

Last night they appeared dark, but today they're full of light, browns and greens swirling together like a painter dipped his brush in both colors and spun it around in a circle on canvas. It reminds me of the trees when I'm underwater, their brown and green outline just a shimmery mass beyond the surface. His deep brown hair isn't quite as shaggy as it was last night—he always gels it into submission for school.

I liked it more when it was wild.

"Thanks a lot," I mutter, tearing my eyes away from him. He's wearing a button-down shirt with a sweater-vest. What does he think this is, prep school? I turn my face away from him and once more rest my cheek on the cool surface of my desk, hoping he'll leave me alone.

"You need anything? A cup of water or an aspirin or something?"

I sit up and glare. Two years since I ran in his clique, and we've hardly spoken. No, that's a lie. They all talk plenty, relentlessly hurling insults my way.

And now I'm supposed to be civil?

"I'll pass." Pain relievers don't work anyway. There's no getting around this. The only relief I'll feel is when I'm in the water tonight. "Don't you have a girl to hit on or something?"

He rolls his eyes. "So you're sticking with the ice-queen thing again this year, huh?"

I blink several times, fighting the urge to defend myself. When Steven was alive, Cole and I never got along. He has this way of calling people out, thinking he knows everything. I guess in two years, he still hasn't changed.

I force my eyes to stare at the whiteboard as the teacher shuffles in and starts writing her name in giant red marker on the top, in big loopy cursive: "Mrs. Jensen."

"Did you have a good summer?"

"Are we really doing this?" I wince as my temple pounds harder. "Just give me the punch line. Have your laugh and move on."

Someone behind us snorts, and I turn to see Sienna, Little Miss Picture-Perfect, sitting down behind me. Why is she sitting there?

She's even worse than Nikki. My eyes dart around the classroom. She's taken the last available seat. Maybe someone will trade with me. Or maybe this teacher does assigned seating. "Oh come on, you know she doesn't talk to people." She stares right at me. "Not even ex–best friends."

Cole lifts an eyebrow. "Funny—she talked to me a few minutes ago."

Is he defending me? Why would he do that? I look over at him, and he gives me a slight smile, showing off his dimple. A stabbing pain to my stomach reminds me why I'm supposed to be mad at him.

"I guess miracles do happen." Sienna shrugs her petite shoulders, her blonde-streaked hair tumbling down her back, and starts digging through one of her many Coach purses. Today it's green, to match the cami she's wearing underneath a white cardigan. Sienna is like that—very matchy-matchy, always pulled together. A picture of lip-glossed perfection. I guess I used to be like that, too. "Do you have an ulcer or something? Your face is all screwed up. It's really not cute," Sienna says. She cocks her head to the side and her platinum hair shimmers, all bounce and body, like she could model for a box of a hair dye.

"I—" I start to say, then stop, snapping my mouth shut. Nothing good comes from talking to my "ex–best friend." Besides, I've been replaced. By Nikki, and Kristi, and Sienna's boyfriend Patrick.

Mrs. Jensen clears her throat, and I turn my attention to the front of the class, promptly ignoring Sienna.

"Now, I know you guys have already had five classes of rules and expectations and agendas, so this shouldn't be anything new, but we'll be going over it anyway."

I grind my teeth. I could have stayed home.

Mrs. Jensen hands out the syllabuses, and I take the last copy and hold it over my shoulder for Sienna without looking at her. When she doesn't immediately take it, I wave it around, as obnoxiously as possible. She yanks it out of my hand, grumbling something underneath her breath.

Mrs. Jensen starts at the top. "This year, we'll cover at least three classics, and three books of your own choice. . . ."

I sigh inwardly. Behind me, Sienna leans in to get closer to Cole, but all it does is amplify her voice in my ear. "So, are you coming to my party?"

I glance around. There has got to be somewhere else to sit. Someone who will trade chairs with me or something. Do I really need to listen to this? To hear everything I'm missing? Two years ago, she would have been asking *me* if I was coming. I would have known she was in this class because we would have shared schedules at seven o'clock this morning, and then squealed when we discovered we had one together.

My eyes sweep the room, take in the same faces as always, but I pause on the desk in the back corner. A new guy, tall and blond and bulky with muscle. I wonder if he's heard the rumors about me yet. I give him until noon before someone warns him to stay away.

He must feel my eyes on him because he turns and catches me staring. I look away, feeling a familiar warmth creep into my cheeks.

I dig a blue pen out of my binder and pretend to be taking notes on Mrs. Jensen's big talk. She's pacing around up there, a fine sheen of sweat glistening on her forehead. I've never heard of her before.

She must be new. Probably straight out of school. She looks like she just graduated from the seventh grade and is all sorts of freaked out about being in front of us all.

I draw little squiggly lines all over the orange paper. They look like waves. Like the ocean. With the orange background, it's like the ocean at sunset—deep blue and orange russet, all mixing together.

At least, that's how I remember the ocean at sunset. I haven't seen it that way since the night Steven died.

"Yeah, can't wait," Cole says.

I slide my chair over just a little bit, trying to avoid listening to this. But two inches isn't enough, and it's all I can manage without drawing attention to myself. The last thing I want is for New Teacher to peg me as a troublemaker.

I feel the urge to look back at Sienna, so I concentrate harder on the paper, the waves growing and filling the empty space at the top, until there's more ink than blank space.

"Everyone is going to be there," Sienna says.

That same feeling stabs me in the chest. Because to her, I'm not *everyone*. I'm no one. She said that on purpose just to get to me.

I glance at the clock. Eight minutes. That's all that's passed since I sat down.

"Awesome. I should be there by eight at the latest." He pauses for a second. "What about you?"

I furrow my brow as I fill in the last blank spot on the left margin of my syllabus. Why is he asking Sienna what time she'll arrive at her own party? When I glance up, I realize that he's asking *me*.

My lips part, but I don't know what to say, and then Sienna jumps in. "As if Lexi's invited."

"I'm busy anyways," I say, but my voice comes out more hollow and sad than I'd anticipated.

Cole's eyes soften and he starts to open his mouth, but I'm saved from his words of pity by the teacher. "You? In the middle? Did you have a question on the grading system?"

My breath catches. "Oh. Uh, no, I think I figured it out. Sorry."

Then I turn back to coloring in the waves, trying to think about the lake tonight and not Sienna's party. I wouldn't go, anyway, so why do I care? I have to go swimming.

Cole better not be at my lake. I can't take another day of agony like this. I need the water like I need air.

When I get home that night, I sink onto the couch, letting out a long slow sigh of relief. I thought today would never end. It's still several hours until dusk, but it feels good to be home, where I don't have to hang on to the facade. I've spent two years training myself to pretend I don't care they all hate me, and it's never gotten easier. These precious hours between school and dusk are the only time I can relax. Once the sun disappears and the moon rises, pulls on the tides—pulls on me—I have to go.

"How was your first day, sweetie?" My grandma walks out of the kitchen, holding a steaming mug with both hands. Tea. Her only addiction.

I sit up. "Good. Tough classes, but I'll be fine."

"You always are. I'm very proud of you, you know." Gram sits down on her recliner and clicks the remote, turning off the television. "Are your friends in any of your classes?"

She takes a slow sip of her tea, staring at me over the lemon-yellow mug with her eyebrows raised. These last two years, she's picked up on the fact that something's changed, but somehow, I've kept my biggest secret, even from her.

She is my father's mother, and she's totally normal, at least as far as I can tell. She doesn't even know how to swim; she used to tell me stories about my father and his sailboat and how she refused to set foot on it until she had a life vest tied firmly around her.

And then one day he sailed away. I always imagined my dad would come back, eventually. That he'd realize it was stupid to leave us. But he never did. Never will.

So, since my Gram isn't big on swimming, that means either I'm a total freak of nature or I got it from my mom. And I'm pretty sure I know which one it is. But my mom's dead. I'll never know for certain.

"Uh, yeah. Sienna is in my English class. Nikki and I have chemistry together." I avoid looking at her and get to my feet. "Did you take your insulin today?" I ask. "What was your reading?"

Gram sets the mug down beside her. "I wish you wouldn't worry so much. That's my job."

I stand in the entry to the kitchen. "I'm not *worried*, Gram. I just like to know that you're not forgetting."

"You set that blasted alarm. How could I forget? I nearly jump out of my chair every time it rings."

I smile, then. "Okay. Good. I'm going to fix you up some more syringes. Want spaghetti for dinner?"

Gram nods, picking up the remote and clicking the television back on. "Sounds good."

I open the fridge and pull out my grandmother's bottle of insulin, then go to the cupboard and take out the box of syringes, a pair of scissors, and a roll of medical tape. I take them to the little dining room table, where my backpack is sitting. I reach into the small zippered pocket and pull out a laminated chart about the size of the average road map.

I lay the chart—the periodic table of elements—out on the table. I spent half the last month preparing for the start of my advanced chem class. We're not required to memorize the periodic table of the elements, but I'm trying to anyway. I'm sure it will help me later.

Knowledge. Books. School. I fill up my head with these things, and it keeps me from going crazy. After staring at the table for a few minutes, I look away, repeating the elements over and over, whispering them under my breath. *Nitrogen, phosphorous, arsenic, antimony, bismuth, ununpentium.*

The fifteenth row.

Carefully, I snip pieces of tape. Seven of them. I label them Monday, Tuesday, Wednesday . . . until the whole week is listed out. Then I take the syringes and load them with 40 cc of insulin. My grandmother's daily dose. I label each syringe and then get up. *Nitrogen, phosphorous, arsenic . . .*

I've already forgotten the rest. I walk to the old, almond-colored fridge, dropping the syringes into the empty box on the top shelf. I stare into the fridge, tapping my nails on the door. Then I reach in and grab some Parmesan cheese and green peppers, my mind turning to the simpler things in life, the things I can control.

I chop the peppers while I bring the water to a boil, listening as *Who Wants to Be a Millionaire* blares in the other room.

My feet are on fire, now, but it's still too early to swim. I don't understand why, but swimming while it's still light out is pointless and unsatisfying. I glance up at the clock.

Three hours to go.

The drive to the lake is excruciatingly long. It's a dozen miles outside town, which would take fifteen minutes to drive if the road were paved. Unfortunately, it's gravel, a rutted, puddle-filled old logging road. My Toyota groans as I climb upward in the darkness, ancient cedar trees soaring out around me, the very trees our town was named for. A light sprinkle has picked up, and my wipers intermittently swipe across the dirty windshield.

The radio in my car doesn't work, so I make the drive every night in silence, my only soundtrack the sounds of my tires crunching on the old gravel surface or the squeaking of the worn-out shocks. When I first started coming here, I used to think it was eerie, driving so far in the silent darkness. But I've grown used to it.

I park under a big fir tree, my car engulfed in shadows. Tonight, the moon is blotted out by the clouds, and a fine mist drizzles down as I step outside my car. I pull on an old fleece jacket and zip it up to my chin, then set out down the trail.

Even without a flashlight, I have no problem navigating the familiar path. Leaves and sticks crunch beneath my worn-out hiking boots. My knees ache as I climb over the trunk of a fallen pine tree. A few more minutes and the pain will go away.

Under the canopy of the evergreen forest, the rain disappears. I unzip my jacket a little and take in a few deep breaths. Looking up through the limbs of the trees, I spot the few stars that aren't hidden by clouds. The slightly sweet, decaying scent of a fallen nurse tree greets me.

Finally, I emerge into the small clearing that surrounds my lake. The instant I see the water, my desire grows. After a night without swimming, it's nearly impossible to keep myself from racing straight to the edge and diving in.

The rain drizzles down, moistening my skin when I step out from under the limbs. I pause at the edge of the shore and look around, straining to hear any snap of twigs or rustle of leaves, but I hear only the sound of the forest. I pull my clothes off and hang them on the same limb as always, and then I walk to the edge of the water. A frog picks up its chorus, and I sigh as I ease into the icy lake. The cool liquid laps at my ankles, and already the pain is melting away.

Maybe Cole didn't like the lake. Maybe he'll never come back.

I wade deeper, then dive into the freezing water when it reaches my waist. Immediately, the muscles in my limbs unwind, my back relaxes. The glacial water is like a warm bubble bath for my body. Everything that happened today is carried away with each kick, each paddle.

I always begin my swim with a few long underwater laps. I can handle nearly ten minutes under the surface, back and forth, before I need more air.

If someone were to see me at exactly the right angle, or if the moonlight hits me just right, they might be able to make out the shimmer of my skin, an almost iridescent glow as I glide through the water. I'm not like Ariel in *The Little Mermaid*. I don't have a tail or anything. Sometimes, my hands brush my legs when I swim, and my skin feels slick, like fish scales. Other times, it feels just like it always does, smooth, regular skin.

It's different during the day. I can still hold my breath for a long time, but my skin doesn't get slick, and I don't get the same relief.

I wish I knew why I crave the water, why I am what I am. But I don't. And I'm not sure I ever will. The only person who could have told me has been gone for six years. At the time my mother died, all I knew was that she'd drowned. That was all my grandmother would tell me. In the years afterward, the ocean's call grew stronger, and I thought it was because my memories of my mother were innately tied to the sea.

I used to spend hours walking the beaches, not sure why I wanted to be so close to the surf. And then came the devastating events of my sixteenth birthday. That's when I finally questioned the story behind my mom's death. After I swam for the first time. After I killed.

It wasn't hard to find out what *really* happened. A quick search on Google, and everything I'd thought about her changed.

It wasn't an accidental drowning, like my grandma said. Her feet were tied to a cinder block. Most of the articles said it was a suicide, and even though I've never wanted to believe it, I don't see how it could be anything else.

The articles always mention another unusual drowning: Greg Roberts, her boyfriend at the time. But Greg wasn't there with her. He died at least twelve hours before she did, a half-mile down the coast.

I knew Greg, but not well. Until I read that article, I'd always thought he'd left town the day my mom died, in some kind of emotional fit. He'd only been with my mom for a year, but their relationship had seemed intense, even to me, a twelve-year-old. My mother could never stop talking about him.

I don't know for sure how he drowned, but after what happened with Steven . . . I have my suspicions. I wish she were still around. I wish she were here to tell me what I am, what it will be like for me in the coming years.

Tonight, I don't think of her for long, because at some point during my swim, my mind goes blank. I surface, and the song— the one I sing every night—bursts out, wrenching free from my throat like I've twisted the cap on a shaken-up bottle of soda. It's a haunting wordless melody that comes from somewhere inside, and I can't control it. My arms paddle steadily, my limbs working together until I'm propelling myself at a pace that would probably trump an Olympic swimmer.

I'm totally checked out as I find my rhythm, switch into autopilot. It reminds me of how it used to feel to sleep, the way the hours pass without a conscious thought. I simply dip into the water and start swimming; and by the time I know it, it's dawn, and I feel refreshed and exhilarated, ready to greet the day.

At dawn, I climb out of the water, my toes sinking into the muddy shore. The soft, squishy earth feels good beneath my feet. The urge to sing is gone, and it won't return for hours. I'm alive, rested, eager to find a way to outsmart the hand I've been dealt.

But moments later, my toes are cold. The chill has seeped into my bones, and reality screeches back. It's unseasonably cool for September. The temperatures in Cedar Cove tend to be mild—although almost constantly rainy and windy—because we're practically *in* the Pacific Ocean. But today, it's barely in the forties.

I'm not ready for the winter. I'm not ready to make it through yet another season of darkness, of long nights and cold mornings with damp hair and even damper skin.

I shiver and for a moment I think about getting back into the lake, but it's dawn, so the water will have no effect on me. I'll just be a normal girl in freezing-cold water, who should be at home in bed.

Even though I never get sick, I don't care for the bone-chilling cold that I feel when I climb out of the water at dawn, my hair dripping down my bare back.

I find the towel I hung on a branch and dry off, then slip back into my clothes. The walk out of the woods takes twenty minutes. The sun rises slowly behind the hilltops, steadily lighting my way. By the time I make it to the road, it's emerged from behind the mountains, full and round and ready for another day. It will take me thirty minutes to drive back to town. So much wasted time, every day, driving and hiking. So much wasted money, filling the beater car every few days. My allowance barely covers the gas.

When I make it to my rusted-out brown Toyota, I turn the key. It sputters briefly, and my heart sinks. But then the engine catches and whirs to life. I promptly crank the heat. Cold air blasts out at me, and I flinch, waiting for it to warm. I sit in the dawn light, the car humming, as my body thaws.

Finally, I shift into gear and begin the descent into Cedar Cove.

CHAPTER THREE

If there were thirty minutes of every day that I could strike from existence, it would be lunchtime. Unfortunately, I have to use the cafeteria scan card to pay for my meals. If I could get my grandmother to give me cash, I would stop at a gas station or the grocery store. I would buy something, *anything*, to avoid those agonizing minutes in the lunch line.

Today, I tap the scan card against the stainless steel countertop, anxious to get my turkey sandwich and leave the cafeteria. The lunch lady is almost done—she's cutting my sandwich in half and putting it on a paper plate.

I grab the plate as soon as she holds it over the counter. Then I take it to the cashier, who quickly scans my card and hands it back. I tuck the card into my back pocket and then head for the door, relief beginning to fill me that the ordeal of getting lunch is almost over.

I realize belatedly that my route may not have been the best choice. Sienna's crowd—all my old friends—claimed a different table this year. My heart climbs into my throat. I'm going to walk right past them.

I slow down and contemplate spinning around, running away. But then I watch as Nikki elbows Kristy Eckly and nods in my direction. In a matter of seconds, they're all staring.

I won't run away. I won't let them see me sweat. I square my shoulders and walk faster, staring straight ahead, focusing everything I have on a vacant look that won't betray my emotions. Fifty feet to freedom. The door beckons in the distance. *So close.*

But I'm so busy trying not to look at them, I don't see something in my path, and I trip. I throw my hands up to catch my balance and my plate slips from my grasp. I manage to keep from falling, but I can't say the same thing for my sandwich—it tumbles to the ground and scatters on the dirty floor.

The whole table snickers and laughs. I refuse to look at them as my face burns and I rush for the door, more careful this time about what's in my path. Just as I reach the exit, I wrench around and glance back. It was a paper sack. I nearly hit the ground over an empty paper bag.

I glance at their table, and my eyes zero in on the one person who isn't laughing. Cole. His face is completely blank, and he's sitting there, perfectly still. As always, girls surround him.

I fling open the door and scurry to the bench in the far corner of the courtyard, the one mostly surrounded by shrubs, where they won't be able to see me from their A-list table in the cafeteria.

Then I pull my legs up on the bench with me and hug my knees.

I rest my forehead on them, closing my eyes and taking in deep breaths to steady my aching heart.

I know they all blame me for killing Steven. I know this is my punishment. Just as I know I deserve it. They blame me because they think I should have saved him somehow, stopped the *senseless tragedy.* If they knew I outright murdered him, I wonder what they'd think, how much worse their taunts would be.

My stomach growls as I sit alone, hoping no one is looking at me but unwilling to glance up to confirm it.

I don't know how long I've been sitting there when a guy clears his throat. I freeze for a second, and then reluctantly uncoil.

Cole stares me straight in the eye. The look he gives me is so different than the ones from the rest of my old friends. His says he doesn't hate me like they do. He sets the plate down, and I stare at the sandwich.

"It's not right."

I swallow. "What?"

"What they do to you."

I tip my head to the side. "They didn't do anything. I'm the idiot who tripped."

"I don't mean just now. I mean . . . every day."

"Why do you even care? It's just the same joke, new year. Nothing I can't handle." I jut my chin up.

"Why do you let them do that? Why do you just take it?"

"Because I deserve it."

He crosses his arms at his chest and looks me dead in the eye. "No one deserves to be treated like dirt."

I glare at him, wishing he'd leave well enough alone. "Yeah. I do. What happened is my fault, and they know it."

"You really blame yourself?"

The silence stretches a beat too long. And then, "Yes."

"Huh." He sighs but doesn't seem to know what to say to this. He shifts his weight, glances back at the cafeteria and then at me again. "Well, enjoy your sandwich."

I want to say something, but there are *so many* things I want to say that I can't seem to articulate anything at all. And then, before I've even had a chance to get a word out, he's stepping away from me, leaving me alone with my guilt. I open my mouth to call out to him, but then I just snap it shut.

No friends. That's my number one rule, the only thing that keeps everyone else safe.

I put my feet back down on the ground and watch him as he crosses the courtyard. A lanky dark-haired girl stops him at the door, giving him a big hug that lingers too long. She says something, and he laughs, and then she walks away, her hips swinging.

He watches her go. I narrow my eyes. He reaches for the door, glancing back at me. He catches me staring and his lips curl into an easy smile.

I look away, down at the sandwich as my stomach growls again. It's the same turkey-on-wheat that I dropped on the floor, except this one isn't wrecked and dirt-covered. I glance back at the cafeteria, but, just like I planned, I can't see their table from this angle.

With a sigh, I pick up the sandwich and take a big bite. I'm so famished that it tastes better than anything I've ever had. The sun warms me through my black shirt as I sit there, chewing quietly on the pity gift from Cole.

I hope the weather holds out for another month or two. It rains almost constantly from October to May in Cedar Cove, Oregon. We're right on the ocean, but the mountains that surround the town trap the clouds right above us.

Then again, when it *really* pours, there are fewer people up in Tillamook Forest; and I don't have to worry as much about someone finding my lake. Today, the sun is out, the sky cloudless. We'll only get a few more weeks of this weather, and then fall will be here, announced by all the leaves turning vibrant shades of crimson and gold, the same as our school colors. By the time football season is half over, it'll barely be forty degrees out, even by midday. I hate the winters, when dusk begins to fall just a couple of hours after school lets out.

And I dread the dusk. The second the moon rises in the night sky, begins its pull on the tides, I'm drawn to the water. In the summer, I only need to swim seven or eight hours per night, but in the winter, when the nights seem to stretch on forever, it's closer to twelve.

I take another bite of the sandwich, staring at the ground.

Nine hours to go, and it's back to the lake.

CHAPTER FOUR

An hour before dusk, I enter Seaside Cemetery, right on time—thirty minutes before dusk, just like always. The cemetery is on a rolling hilltop ten minutes south of Cedar Cove, not far from the bluffs. The sweeping, beautiful million-dollar views of the Pacific stretch out below me.

I walk down the winding concrete pathways, past the big, soon-to-be bare weeping willow, and to the fourth grave after the tree. Steven's. Once there, I drop to my knees next to the stone, between the body of Steven Goode and his neighbor's, a guy named Mathew Pearson. A guy who'd been blessed with sixty-two years on this earth, more than three times as many as Steven had.

I turn around and lie back on the grass, staring toward the cloudless September sky. As the pinks and oranges of sunset begin to seep into the sky, I can't help but think about what dusk means. If

Steven were lying on top of the grass, instead of six feet under, he'd be right next to me. We could spend the next half-hour touching shoulders, intertwining our fingers. The chill of the grass would disappear under the warmth of his smile.

Instead, he's cold and dead, buried beneath the ground in a beautiful mahogany coffin that cost his mother eight thousand dollars.

"Hey, Steven," I say. I dig into my pocket and produce a tiny Hot Wheels Chevelle. It's electric blue, like his was. "I found this at a toy store the other day." I hold it up to the sky, as if he'll be able to see it from wherever it is his soul resides.

"I know it's not the same thing. I mean, you can't drive it or anything. But it made me think of you, so . . ." *I bought one for you and kept one for me.*

My voice trails off, and I drop my arm back to my side. "The guy who bought your car lives in town, you know. I see him sometimes. He's, like, fifty. I bet he has no idea how hard you worked to restore it. Stinks that you can't be the one to enjoy it."

My voice cracks and catches in my throat. This is the only time of day I let my guard down. I'm not sure why I come up here every day, as if I'll find the answers, as if he'll tell me he doesn't blame me for what happened. But somehow talking to him takes a tiny piece of the guilt away. It's just a little ice chip of a huge iceberg, but it's something.

I swallow as the first tear brims and rolls across my temple. As my vision swims with tears, it makes the darkening sky look like the ocean, like rippling, shimmering water.

And suddenly, I'm there again, standing on the dark beach with Steven.

I giggle when he slips his arms around my waist, nervous. We've been dancing around this for weeks. I've been too afraid to ask him what he was waiting for. Too afraid I was wrong.

But tonight everything is different. Tonight we stopped dancing.

I watch the water roll in to shore, Steven behind me, his lips brushing across the crook of my neck. There's something in the air tonight, something electric that seems to be setting me on fire. It's a humid late-summer night, the dark clouds threatening rain that never seems to come. All they do is blot out the moon and the stars and make it hard to see more than a dozen yards ahead.

The air tastes like salt, like summer, like everything I love, and the urge to get in and swim is overwhelming.

I twist around in his arms, until I'm facing him. He leans down, and the kiss is long, lingering. I can't believe we're really here, really doing this. It's like something from a dream. I find myself backing up without breaking the kiss, until I feel the sea lapping at my feet. Steven pulls away for a second, surprised by the feel of it, but I yank him back down to me, wanting more.

More, more, more. That's all I can think. The need is overwhelming. "Let's go swimming," I whisper between kisses. I don't know why I want to swim, but I do. Desperately. And before he can react, I'm pulling his T-shirt over his head and throwing it onto the beach.

Steven blinks. Maybe I'm moving too fast after waiting so long. But he wants it, too—I can see that. He watches as I toss my shirt with his. And when I pull my pants off, he does the same. And then we're standing there, in our underwear. I grab his hand and lead him further into the water.

I'm nervous, but I don't care, and I can't seem to stop myself from dragging him deeper.

I'm always so cautious, so carefully controlled. But tonight I'm reckless, taking what I want without regard for the consequences.

An overwhelming sense of desire spirals inside me as our feet leave the sandy bottom. He goes to kiss me, but a wave splashes into us. We throw back our heads and laugh.

I'm giddy and euphoric, so exquisitely happy it's uncontainable.

I laugh again and flip onto my back to float and paddle out further. Steven's saying something, but the water filling my ears makes it impossible to decipher. I laugh again, and it comes out strange, melodic. It bubbles out and changes, fills the night air with a hauntingly beautiful song.

It can't be me, singing it, but it is. The notes ring out, stronger and stronger as I pick up an urgent paddle. I don't know why I'm doing this; I only know it feels right. As if I've waited my entire life to sing this song.

Soon, I stop thinking altogether, my arms paddling steadily, until I'm propelled faster and faster, gliding along more rapidly than any other creature in the water. Vaguely, I know Steven is out here with me, but I can't seem to think clearly. The song grows, intensifying, louder, vibrating in my chest.

But abruptly, as I reach for another stroke, the melody dies in my throat. Silence rings out.

Suddenly, the urge to sing is gone. My head clears, the fog lifting all at once.

What am I doing? Where did Steven go?

I swim upright, treading water, trying to make out the beach in the distance. Did he get out? Swim to shore? *I peer into the darkness, but it's impossible to see beyond twenty feet. The swells rise around me, and I bob along the surface, waiting.*

The desire to swim has vanished. The memory, now faint, of my laughter twisting into a strangely wordless song rattles me. I want to get out, and I can't seem to remember why it seemed so important to swim in the first place. It's nearly midnight, and a storm is sure to roll in soon.

I flip onto my back and kick my way to the shore. I knock into something with my head, so hard it seems to echo inside my skull. Quickly, I right myself, get my feet underneath me.

The inky darkness makes it impossible to see what is floating in front of me. I reach out, the water rippling with my movements. At first, I'm not sure what I feel beneath my fingers. But then, I know.

Hair.

Skin.

I jerk back, so fast I bob under and inhale a mouthful of water. I have to kick hard to keep my mouth above water as I cough and gasp.

I reach out again, my heart thundering in my chest, my hand trembling as I pull the body around, squinting into the darkness.

It's . . .

Steven.

A scream rips free of my throat and, for a moment, I'm frozen. My legs no longer kick. I slowly sink. But then I cough up more seawater, and it occurs to me to tread. I watch his body bob along the surface, the waves swelling around us.

My mind clears and spurs me into motion. I hook an arm around his chin and kick hard, propelling myself toward the shoreline. I glide through the water faster than any human could possibly swim, faster than I ever knew I could. It seems to be just seconds before I am hauling him up onto the sand.

But he hasn't moved, hasn't struggled in my arms.

No. No, no, no, no.

I lean over and try to breathe life into him. I plug his nose and give him everything I have. I press on his chest, trying to force his heart to beat. He can't be that far gone. He can't be. It seemed like only seconds we were apart.

I desperately pound on his chest, try to force the air into his lungs, but it doesn't work. Tears clog my throat.

"Steven!" I scream at him, pound at his chest, sobbing.

His eyes are blank, glassy. Haunting.

I lean over and cry. For everything he was. For everything we'll never be.

A truck rumbles by on the street above us, so loud I jump back. It brings reality screeching with it.

Help. Someone can help.

I scramble up the sandy bank, reed grass slicing into my bare feet, until I'm standing under a streetlamp. The night air is no longer warm on my bare, wet skin. The rain that has threatened for days sprinkles down as I step foot onto the pavement.

Headlights swing toward me as a car comes from around the bend. I stumble into the middle of street, waving my hands above my head. The lights beam right onto me, blinding me, until I have to shield my eyes. I must look crazed, soaking wet and half naked.

And then a spotlight joins it and the lights flash red and blue.

It's a cop.

I play it over and over in my mind, every day of my life, but every time it ends the same. I'm wrapped up in a blanket in the backseat of a police car as Steven's cold, sheet-covered body is wheeled past me. The bed jostles as they lift it into the ambulance, and his hand slides out from under the sheet, and all I can see is his pale, lifeless fingers.

I blink, hard, washing away the memory. You don't have to sleep, you don't have to dream, to have nightmares.

His death was considered suspicious. He was a vibrant seventeen-year-old athlete who shouldn't have succumbed to the waves—he swam in his family's pool every day and surfed during the summer. The police never understood why we went swimming on such a dark night; and at the time, neither did I.

I was brought in for questioning again and again. I retold the story over and over—leaving out the part where I sang. Even then, before I really understood what that meant, I knew not to mention it.

Eventually, the police determined that there was no way I could have drowned him myself. At least not by any normal means. Steven was so much bigger than me, so much stronger. When the autopsy came back clean—no bruising, no skin underneath his fingernails, no sign of a struggle—the drowning was ruled accidental.

Reporters speculated that he'd become disoriented in the dark. Unable to find the shore, he simply got too tired to keep his head above water. Others said it must have been a leg cramp, worsened by the growing waves. A sad, tragic accident.

But my friends never saw it that way. They wanted to know why I led him out of the house, toward the beach. Why I didn't save him. And when I refused to explain anything, even to Sienna, they turned on me.

In the days following his death, I ignored the intense desire to swim, and I shut everyone out. I pulled the drapes closed in my room and lay there all night long, staring at the shadows, pretending I wasn't craving the feel of the water against my skin.

With each day, I grew sicker. It was just a little fever at first, but soon I could hardly stand it. Eventually, I drove up to an old lake where I used to go swimming with Sienna and Nikki and Kristi.

I sang all night. And by morning, I felt stronger than ever. But the feeling only lasted a day.

Within two weeks, I was swimming every night.

I sigh, rolling over onto my stomach and propping myself up on my elbows. Maybe it's morbid to be lying here in the grass, just six feet above the bodies. Maybe someone would be horrified if they saw me. But I need this time with him—it's the only thing that keeps me sane. Luckily, Steven's grave is hard to see from the pathways because of a few shrubs and the willow. I would probably see someone long before they'd see me.

I reach out and trace my fingers over Steven's grave marker. *Steven Goode. Beloved Son, Brother and Friend.* At the bottom is an engraved football. Steven didn't even like football. I never told anyone that. He did it for his dad, who played through high school and college but never made it pro. That was when I first began to hope that he liked me—he was telling me secrets no one else knew. Secrets he trusted me with.

I never got to tell him mine. I spent three years pining for him; just when things started to shift, just when it looked as if the romance wasn't all in my head, I killed him.

I set the Chevelle in front of his headstone. Every night, I tell him everything, even about the curse I live with. He's the only one who knows the truth. Unless I want all my old friends to end up in the ground next to him, I have to keep them away.

I kiss my fingertips and then place them on his headstone. For a brief moment, my fingers linger on the marble, and I wonder for the thousandth time what it would have been like to *be* with him for more than just a moment. My sixteenth-birthday party could have been the start of something. And instead, it was the end.

I wonder for the thousandth time if he could have loved me in that same fierce way I loved him. "Good night, Steven."

I get up and wipe my knees off and then step back onto the pathways. It's getting darker now and harder to see. I have another night of swimming ahead of me. Even as I leave his body to rot in a grave that I put him in, I must return to the water.

"See you tomorrow," I whisper, as if someone will hear.

And then I take the first few steps that will leave him behind.

CHAPTER FIVE

I swam all night, but my stomach still churns as I walk into the doors at school, zipping up my fleece jacket as though somehow it will protect me from what's to come. Getting through today will be a gauntlet.

We're two weeks into the school year, now, which means one thing: it's my birthday. It should be a happy day. For any other person in this school, it would be. But my birthday will forever mark the anniversary of Steven's death; and no one is going to let me forget it. The police may have cleared my name, but to everyone else, I was found guilty. Forever and always, the one who stole Steven from their lives.

I tip my chin up, square my shoulders, and try to walk to my locker as if I don't notice the watchful eyes of my classmates.

An underclassman, oblivious to the tension in the hall, walks by me, his eyes sweeping over me in an appreciative, almost lustful way before he catches my glare and turns away.

A group of people, Sienna and her boyfriend Patrick, plus Nikki and Kristi, stand together not far from my locker. They lounge around a big bay window, officially reserved for seniors. *Unofficially,* it's for top tier seniors, and that means it belongs to them. Why did I have to be cursed with a locker so close to their stomping grounds?

I turn to my locker, concentrating on keeping my hand from shaking so much they'll see it. I screw up the combination the first time and have to start over. I can feel their eyes on my back, watching me. My chest tightens and it seems harder to breathe.

Finally, I hit the last digit and pop the door open.

Sand spills out in a wave, piling up at my feet. My books, my papers, everything is filled with grit.

I whirl around, wondering which of my classmates is to blame. Sienna's closer than before, her hand on her hip. She's wearing a knee-length black skirt and one of Steven's old T-shirts, the one he used to wear at least once a week. I haven't seen that shirt since last year. Since my *seventeenth* birthday. I wonder what else of his she's kept.

My chest rises and falls rapidly, and I'm so close to losing it I want to just leave everything like this and run.

"Happy birthday," she says, her voice trembling.

I blink.

There's no anger to her words.

I clench my hands, desperate to hold it together. "How long are you going to do this?"

She tilts her head to the side and the light streaming in from their window catches the tears shimmering in her eyes. "Until I get my brother back."

She spins around and walks away. I want to scream at her that I want him back as much as she does, that I never wanted to kill him and she doesn't have to keep doing this to me, but I swallow the words.

One by one, the crowd disperses. I turn back to my locker, slam it shut, and stalk off in the opposite direction.

Happy birthday to me.

When I walk in the door at home, my gram is in her recliner, but her eyes are shut, and the steady sawing of her snoring fills the living room. I pause in the faded hardwood entry and watch her, my hands still gripping my heavy backpack.

Her gray hair is rumpled, her matching pink sweats and sweatshirt a little wrinkled, but she's never looked more serene. I wish I could look that peaceful. Every limb, every muscle is relaxed.

I turn away and go to the kitchen, flinging open a few cupboards. Dinner. It will occupy my hands and my mind. I survey the options for a long moment, my arms crossed. I'm not in the mood to cook anything elaborate. I only want to get the meal over with, smile in a convincing way, and retreat to my room to wait out the hours until dusk. I grab beans, corn, some dry noodles, and stewed tomatoes. I'll throw it all together with a little bit of frozen vegetables and call it soup. Gram loves soup.

I fill a pot with water and set it on the stove, twisting the dial to high. As I pull a ladle out of the drawer, a flash of pink catches my eye. I smile as big as I can manage at my grandmother as she shuffles toward me, hoping to hide the strain of my day at school.

"Lexi, honey, I didn't hear you come in."

"You were sleeping, Gram."

She frowns. "You shouldn't have to cook dinner on your birthday."

"I know, but I like cooking." I dump the noodles into the pot and then turn back to look at her. "It's okay, really. You can sit down. It'll be ready in twenty minutes."

She shuffles away from me down the hall, her slippers swishing on the hardwood. I watch her until the bright pink disappears.

I twist back around and reach for the can opener, humming to myself as I open up the tomatoes and dump them into the pot. Everything about school sucks, but I find comfort in the normalcy of being at home. It's so different from my intense, supernatural problems. When I'm here, I don't have to watch my back.

I find the Italian seasoning jar in the cupboard and pour a bunch in. Then I lean a hip against the counter as I watch the soup come to a boil.

The shuffling returns. My grandmother's face is hidden by a big box wrapped in plain brown paper. Her wrinkled, veiny hands grip it tightly.

My mouth goes dry. "I thought we agreed no gifts," I say. I refuse to take anything but the gas money I so desperately need.

"This isn't from me," she says, placing it on the counter.

When I see the handwriting on the top, my mouth goes dry.

"It's from your mother. She gave it to me before . . ." Her voice trails off, and then she clears her throat. "She wanted me to give it to you."

I frown. "You've kept this for six years?"

"I was afraid it would upset you too much to have her old things. But you're an adult now. If you want to see them, they're yours."

"Oh." I stare at the package.

She puts a hand on mine. "I'll finish up this soup. Why don't you go to your room and open it in private?"

This time I don't resist. I take the package and retreat to my room, closing the door behind me with a quiet click.

Six years, my grandmother has kept this.

I perch at the edge of my bed, on top of my mom's old flowery comforter. It seems like a lifetime ago that I lived with her in a rental house on the other side of town.

I stare at the box for several long seconds. I'm afraid to discover what's inside. What if it's something stupid, like a jewelry box or stuffed teddy bear?

What I need is answers, something that tells me what I'm supposed to do, how I'm supposed to fix the lives I've ruined.

I reach out and tear the paper off. My heart beats louder in my ears. The box is heavy as I rip open the lid and reach in. My fingers find a scrap of paper, and I pull it out, unfolding it as I take in a long breath.

For my daughter, on her sixteenth birthday.
My only regret is not being here for you today when you need me. I hope this will help you understand what is to come.

I don't realize I'm crying until a dark splotch appears on the paper. It was supposed to be for my *sixteenth* birthday. The day everything changed. Did my grandmother know that and forget? Or did my mother not make it clear?

I read the note again.

My mom knew. She knew she was going to leave me, and she wrote this note, four years before I was supposed to read it.

Did she write it before or after she killed Greg?

I reach in and touch something hard and leathery, and as I pull it out, I realize it's a book. A very old book.

My fingers trail over the dry, fading surface as I pull it onto my lap, the dust covering my jeans. It must be ancient. As I lift open the cover, the spine cracks.

The first aged, yellowed page is nearly blank, except for three words written in stark, perfect calligraphy:

For the cursed.

I take in a jagged breath of air, then slide my finger over the page and flip it over.

January 7, 1750

William doesn't belong with Julia. Their betrothal is a business arrangement, nothing more. Now that he is in love with me, he wants to marry me, and not her. He has promised me he will end their engagement.

I suppose she does not care much what he wants, for it is William's title she is after, and she will fight for that if he tries to jilt her. I hope he remains strong.

Tonight, when he dared dance with me at the Harksbury ball,

I saw it in her eyes. I knew before the song was over that I had committed a sin. Afterward, I stood by, humiliated, as he lied to soothe her. He told her he was only being polite. Told her no one had asked me to dance and so, as a gentleman, he had asked me.

A pity dance.

And yet still she seethed, and I knew something had shifted between us.

She will do anything to have him, anything to become a duchess. That is why we must elope. Will has asked me to wait one month, and then he will be mine, and only mine.

Charlotte

January 18, 1756

I am terrified. Julia knows. She knows everything. She found me packing my bags, and she confronted me. She thinks just because I am her paid companion that she can control everything about me, but she cannot decide who I will love.

She told me I was a fool to believe him. She told me he compromised her and is duty bound to marry her. Her words left a dull ache in my chest. She must be lying. It is I who has been compromised. But I am little more than a servant. He cannot be forced to marry me. For the first time, I am not sure I have done the right thing these last months.

But I must trust in him. He loves me. He will honor all of his whispered promises. There is nothing I can do but believe in it for it is too late to go back and undo the things I have done.

Charlotte

February 7, 1750

Will was supposed to arrive last night to take me away. I sat on an overturned bucket behind the stables for three hours, shivering against the cold, and yet he did not arrive. I had to beg a groom to saddle a horse so that I could go to his estate. And yet it was useless because they said he has gone hunting up north with friends. How could he do such a thing at a time like this?

I was forced to go back home, but Julia soon discovered where I had gone. She came at me in a rage, and if not for her father's valet, I might very well have been injured. Her father dismissed me not an hour later without references.

This afternoon, I stood on the stoop awaiting the carriage that would take me away from the only home I have known these last two years, when Julia positively flew up the drive on horseback, her hair undone and streaming behind her. I had never seen her so unkempt, and the look in her eyes was enough to put my stomach in knots.

She leapt from her horse and threw something at me. Some shimmery, dusty powder, which sent me into a coughing fit. It still burns in my lungs as I write this, miles away at a shabby inn.

It was a gypsy curse, she claimed. Her eyes were wide and frightening as she told me I would be as lonely and miserable as she was then. That I would pay for trying to steal her betrothed. I tried to tell her it was he who pursued me, but she would have none of it.

I have little to my name, but so long as Will keeps his promises to me, all will be right.

Charlotte

February 15, 1750

I have been unable to find Will. He has been away from his home for more than a week. I have rented a small room over a tavern, as it was all I could afford. I am but a few miles from Will's home, just down the coast, near the Exmoor Cliffs. I had originally planned to travel inland, but I could not bear to leave the sea behind. Odd, as I had always loathed the smell of the salt in the air.

Charlotte

The lump in my throat grows. This is it. This is how it all started. Two hundred and fifty years ago. My fingers tremble as they slide across the curled yellow paper. I flip the page.

March 21, 1750

I found myself in the sea last night, swimming for no reason at all. I am lucky I did not drown for I have never learned how to swim. I want to go home, but I do not have a home anymore, and I must remember that.

I think I may be with child, and I do not know what to do. I have sent two letters for Will, but he has not answered. I suspect Julia is somehow intercepting my correspondence.

Charlotte

March 30, 1750

I cannot stay here any longer as I am nearly out of funds and I will be thrown out on the street soon. I must travel south to find my cousin and pray that she will take me in.

But I will not leave just yet. I cannot bear to go without seeing Will again. I am going to Varmoth Manor one last time in the hopes that he has returned.

I must know if he will truly marry Julia as the papers say.

Charlotte

April 2, 1750

He is dead. I've done something terrible. I do not understand what has happened to me, but I must flee.

Julia did something to me. I should have known by the crazed look of her she was desperate, that she'd done something so much worse than I had believed.

I must find her immediately. Before I am hanged for murder. I am but a servant and he a duke. They will not rest until they uncover the truth.

Until they uncover me.

Charlotte

I flip the page, but there are no more entries in Charlotte's dark, angled cursive. I flip back and forth a few times, trying to figure out what happened.

The next dates are from late 1766. These entries are written in a different handwriting, lighter, curlier than Charlotte's. I turn back to her entries and do the math.

Sixteen years. There's a sixteen year gap. I hold my breath as my eyes scan the first entry.

It's Charlotte's daughter. Will's daughter. Cursed to the same fate. My chest tightens and I stop midsentence. I flip several pages, until I spot a new script. This time, it's eighteen years later. A new girl. Same story. She recaps the last couple of years on the first page. She tells about the first one she killed.

I flip back a few pages. Why did Charlotte stop writing? Did she die, or simply pass the book along to her daughter?

My fingers flip faster and faster as the writing changes again and again and again. I can't bear to read the stories, not today. I expect they'll all be painfully familiar.

Just as I am about to slam the book shut, I glimpse the final set of entries.

My mother's handwriting stares back at me.

The entry isn't dated on top, like the others, but rather scribbled to the side, as if done in haste. It's over sixteen years old. I wasn't even two yet when she wrote it.

I jerk back. It's the year my father left us. It's hard to breathe over the lump in my throat as I take in the words on the page.

> *I told him the truth. I thought that he loved me, that he would stay. If not for me, then for Lexi. But he couldn't stand the sight of me once he learned what I am. He was gone within hours, while she still slept. He never even told her good-bye.*

I blink. My father. She's talking about my father.

> *I'll never show someone my true nature again. This is pain like I've never felt. Rejection.*

I grind my teeth hard in a desperate attempt to keep the tears at bay. The page is ripped on three of the four edges, as if it had once been longer, but this is all she was willing to save. All she was willing to share for all eternity, with the other girls who would eventually read the book.

I flip the page.

> I've done the one thing I thought I'd never do. I've killed.
>
> I didn't know Greg had followed me. I didn't know he was there, in the shadows, as I stepped into the ocean.
>
> It doesn't matter how it happened, all that matters is he's gone. And I'm the one who killed him. It was nearly impossible to let go of his hand, even after it grew cold. I left him there at the edge of the tides for someone else to find.
>
> This pain hurts more than anything I could have imagined, far more than mere rejection. It is impossible to live with.
>
> I want to be there for Lexi, but I can't go on. I'm no stronger than the others who came before me. I'll never be happy because I'll always be a siren.
>
> Lexi, when you read this, please know that my only regret is leaving you.

I sob, a great, choking thing that racks my shoulders. Collapsing into a ball, I push the book off me. It hits the floor with a loud thunk.

I suppose I knew all along my mother killed herself, but seeing it like this, so black and white, is devastating. It was her decision to tie that cinder block to her feet, to leap from the pier.

And hers is the same pain that I live with every day.

What if I'd had this book two years ago? Would I have gone swimming with Steven? I'd like to think no. Never. But I'm not sure if that's true.

For two hundred and fifty years, every generation gave birth to another girl like me. And every girl lured another man to his death. It was inevitable, my killing Steven.

I know what I am now, what I'll always be—a siren.

I clutch my knees to my chest and sob even harder, hoping my grandmother can't hear me.

CHAPTER SIX

I walk through the double doors at school, tightening my grip on the straps of my plain black backpack. I'm only a few feet into the hall when it all goes bad. My foot hits something and I fly across the entry. I scramble to stop myself, but all I can do is throw my arms up and brace for impact. My elbows skin on the ugly brown carpet, burn with pain.

I realize belatedly what tripped me: a foot in my path. Someone did it on purpose.

I end up sprawled out, facedown, my backpack thrown forward. I pick up my head. Everyone is staring. Physically, though, I'm okay.

My binder doesn't fare so well. My assignments and notes are all scattered, strewn across the floor.

I look up again at a sea of my former friends. Sienna, Nikki,

Kristi, half of Steven's former football teammates. Two years ago, they would have had my back if someone had done this to me. It would have been *them* to help me to my feet, to collect my things.

Instead, they just stand there, smirking. Some even laugh and whisper.

But I won't let them see that they're getting to me. I rip my gaze away and take in long, calming breaths. I focus on my anger. On the asshole who must have tripped me.

But it doesn't matter how hard I try to hide it: they do get under my skin. Not because of their taunts, so much. But because they know the truth, that I'm responsible for Steven's death. Everything they do to me just reminds me of what I did to *him*.

I grit my teeth as people begin to turn away, the entertainment officially over. They tread on my binder, shredding my trig homework and leaving dirty footprints in their wake. I snatch up what remains of my homework and shove it into my binder.

Suddenly, a hand appears in front of me, holding a stack of my chemistry notes. My eyes trail from the hand, up to the arm, then shoulder, then neck . . . until I'm staring up at Cole's face. He looks concerned. "I think these belong to you."

I look up at him, forcing all emotion from my own face. I stifle a *thank you* as I stand up, rip the papers from his hands, and shove them inside my bag. For a split second, I let my gaze linger on his.

Then I spin around and stalk off.

Several hours later, I sit in English class, fidgeting in my seat. Sienna and Cole sit too close for comfort. Everyone does.

I wish they would all simply forget my existence. I wish I could forget them, too, but it's impossible to forget my former life. I ache for the friends I once had, because I know that I can never have them again.

I have to deny myself friends. It's the only way I'll stay alive. The only way *they'll* stay alive.

And it's not like they want me back anyway. At Steven's funeral, Cole tried to talk to me, but I wasn't ready to talk to *anyone*. And then seconds later, Sienna showed up, told me I had no right to be there, and, in a final display of emotion, slapped me.

Cole grabbed her by the waist and hauled her away, screaming; and by the next time I saw her at school, she'd withdrawn, created a cool, detached image that fools everyone. Everyone but me.

Mrs. Jensen hands back my graded homework for the first two weeks, jolting me from my trip down memory lane. I look at the marks.

A

A

A

I smile a little as I slide the graded essays into the back pocket of my mostly reassembled binder. If the rest of life could just be as easy as homework. It's almost as effortless as swimming.

Mrs. Jensen returns to the front, dusting her hands off on her jeans. "So now that that's done, let's get right into our first big project."

A few students groan, but I perk up. Even though I don't look forward to *school,* I like my classes. Someday, I'm going to be a doctor or a research scientist. I'll find the cure for cancer or something. I'll give back to this world the things I've taken.

I'll go away for college, somewhere far away and big enough that I can be anonymous, blend into the student body. Sure, I'll have to find somewhere else to swim, but I'll worry about that when I come to it.

"Your first project will be done in groups."

Murmurs spread throughout the room as students attempt to snag partners. My heart sinks, even as I try to remind myself this is part of working toward something bigger than the curse. Maybe I can work with that new guy, Erik something-or-other. Maybe he hasn't heard the rumors about me yet, even though we've already had weeks of classes.

Mrs. Jensen clears her throat to silence the rumblings. "Before you get too excited, I will be *assigning* groups of three. So let's see. . . ." Mrs. Jensen begins dividing the room up. As she reaches our corner of the room, the horrible, inevitable truth dawns: I'm going to end up with Sienna and Cole.

No. This can't happen. I can't talk to her. I can't talk to *him.*

Just as I expected, she names the three of us off and then turns back to the board, as if she hasn't just drastically altered the course of the universe, or at the very least, sparked off the third world war. I grip the edges of my table and struggle to breathe.

"For your project, I'd like you to read and discuss a novel. You may choose any book you'd like, but you'll need to submit your selection for approval by tomorrow. Your assignment will be to complete an interpretive project for the class, which must include both a paper and a presentation. There are three of you, so I expect some good results."

The class begins shuffling their desks around. I wait a few

moments longer than I should and then grab the edges of mine and spin around, until I'm staring at Sienna's hostile face. I glance at Cole. His sweet, unassuming smile catches me off guard. How can he look so relaxed when he knows what it's like between Sienna and me?

"I'm thinking fantasy," I say through gritted teeth. "Maybe one of Eva Stonewall's novels."

"Do you even know how *weird* you are sometimes? You look like you swallowed denture glue."

"What's that? I couldn't hear you because your prepster shirt is so loud," I say. Her eyes flutter momentarily as she glances down at the bright pink and yellow V-neck she's wearing. She glares at me.

Cole glances between us but ignores our verbal smack down. "Those are girlie books. How about something by Carl Levison?"

"Ick. His books are boring," Sienna says. "If you've read one, you've read them all."

"Are you kidding me? That man's a genius," Cole says.

Sienna shrugs. "Let's do *Manhattan Prep*."

I snort. "Leave it to you to choose something trashy like *Manhattan Prep*. Mrs. Jensen will never let us do that—it's right up there with comic books."

Sienna rolls her eyes at me and crosses her arms. "Not if we play it right. We can tell Mrs. Jensen we plan to explore whether the books are an intentionally satirical view of the privileged. Maybe the author's true motivation is to show how shallow the elite really are by exaggerating the behavior of the characters. She's mocking them, not glamorizing them."

Cole doesn't hesitate in countering her. "There's no way those books are meant as satire. They're just trashy soap-opera novels. Mindless drivel." All of a sudden, he pauses. His eyes light up and he sits up straighter. "What if we use that format for our presentation? We can stage a debate for the class—are the books meant to be tongue-in-cheek, or are they nothing more than trash?"

Sienna crosses her arms. "Uh-uh. We can do a normal presentation, one where we separately memorize our parts. No . . ."—her voice trails off, and she glares at me—"interaction required."

"Come on. I thought you were valedictorian?" Cole says.

She snorts. "I *am* valedictorian."

Cole gives her a pointed look. "Prove it. We do something unexpected, something inventive, and we'll nail this."

Sienna huffs, her need to succeed outweighing her desire to avoid me. "Whatever."

Cole leans back against his chair, a smug expression on his face.

I turn away and stare at the scribbles of permanent marker on the corner of my desk, trying in vain to keep the panic at bay. I can't do this. I can't work with her. With them.

When I look up, Cole is grinning at me, sending my heart scrambling. "You in?"

I smile weakly, nod, and yank my desk away, counting down the seconds until I can slip into my lake tonight.

CHAPTER SEVEN

That night, I sit at the dinner table across from my grandmother. Behind me, the wood stove crackles, warming my backside. I pick up a pretzel twist from the bowl in between us and chew off the pieces of salt. Gram reaches out, sliding four tiles up next to an *S. BOATS*. How ironic.

She looks at me as she lines it up on the Scrabble board, and for a second I think she's going to say something, but she doesn't.

"Do anything fun today?" I ask.

She chews on her lip while she reaches into the plastic bag and draws her replacement letters. "Oh, not really. One of my exercise sessions at the center. How about you?"

I stare at my tiles. I drew a bunch of consonants, and only one vowel—a *U*. The fire crackles again as a log splits, and the light of the room turns a little more orange. "We got a new assignment in

English. It's a group thing. We have to read a novel, and then we're going to debate about it in front of the class."

"Oh?" She raises a brow.

I spell out *HURRY* on the board and take a measly handful of points. My grandmother isn't very good at this game, but I like letting her win. It's a careful balance not to give away my ploy.

"Yeah. The teacher paired me with Sienna and Cole."

She fiddles with her tiles, arranging and rearranging them on her little tray. "Well that worked out nicely, being in a group with your friends." She raises her eyes to meet mine, and I try not to react. I look down at the bag and grab a few replacement tiles, hoping my evasiveness doesn't give me away.

Lately, she's been getting suspicious. It began this summer, when she realized I was alone the entire time, reading college textbooks and watching Discovery Channel documentaries. I told her Sienna spent the whole break in France with her family. It worked, for a while, until she ran into Sienna's mom at the bank. Leave it to her to remember the one thing I wish she'd forget. I had to scramble and make something up, about how they must have come home early, but I still don't know for sure if she bought it.

"Yeah, it's cool. The project should be an easy A."

"How are the rest of your classes?"

I shrug. "Same as usual. Some really good teachers, some meh."

She nods, finally spelling out *PORK*. "You should do a movie night soon, like you used to when you were younger. Have Sienna over, get some of your favorite buttered popcorn." She looks up at me, her eyes appraising, studying my reaction. She might be forgetful but she's not stupid.

I fight the urge to swallow as I know she'll catch on. "Yeah. That would be fun."

"Great. Talk to her about it and I'll take care of the rest. Well, you two should probably pick the movie."

"Uh-huh. Sure." I nod again and spell out *PATIO*.

My grandmother smiles triumphantly as she uses the rest of her tiles to spell out *ORDAINED*. She waves her hand across the board with a flourish. "I win!"

In more ways than one, I think.

The following day, Mrs. Jensen gives us time to work on our projects in class. I wish she wouldn't. Maybe then I could just e-mail some debate points to Cole, and he could do a few and send them to Sienna, and we could avoid talking until debate day. I still can't believe an English teacher would let us choose *Manhattan Prep* at all, but I guess Mrs. Jensen was intrigued by the debate idea.

It's so hard to be around Sienna and not think about everything we shared growing up. Not think about laughing so hard we spit soda all over her dining room table. Not think about the first time her mom dropped us off at the mall by ourselves and we felt so adult buying our back-to-school clothes without parental guidance.

How can it be two years now since we shared that stuff?

The three of us push our desks together, and Sienna pulls out a dog-eared copy of *Manhattan Prep*. Cole digs out his own copy and sets it down on the desk. I can tell he bought it recently, because it has the newer cover with the cast from the TV show, instead of the original.

"Please tell me someone saw you buying that," I say. I attempt to look haughty and snobbish, but I wonder if I'm pulling it off. He doesn't look at me like everyone else does. I feel stripped bare every time he's close.

Cole doesn't take my insult seriously. "Nope. I borrowed it from my sister," he announces, grinning.

Sienna sets down two piles of note cards, one pink and one yellow. Most of them have her loopy, feminine handwriting all over them. "We can put the pros on one color and cons on the other. Like a point-counterpoint thing."

"Whatever," I say. "You guys debate. I'll be the moderator."

Sienna shuffles the cards like she's starting a poker tournament. "No way. We have to contribute equally, and if I"—she pauses and points at herself with one of her perfectly French-manicured nails— "have already done half the planning, then you"—she points at me—"are doing the debate. You and Cole can duke it out on who gets pro *Manhattan Prep,* who gets anti."

I want to thunk my head against my desk. It's like she's trying to punish me. This stupid debate wasn't even my idea, and now I have to stand in front of the class and participate.

Instead, I say, "Who died and made you queen?"

Too late, I realize it was the wrong thing to say in every way imaginable and nearly choke, trying to undo it.

Sienna leans forward and stares straight at me, pursing her lips into a thin line and narrowing her eyes. From here, I can see every mascara-clad lash. "You did."

I stare back at her, those two tiny words ringing over and over again in my head. Because they're true. I am as good as dead to all these people. Years ago, I was practically royalty to my classmates, but after Steven, Sienna took over the reins, along with Nikki. They're the ones who decide which clothes are acceptable, which parties matter.

She looks away and stares at her nails, as if she's bored of this conversation. "Do you know what the government used to do to traitors?"

I just stare back at her, immobile, afraid of where she's going.

She turns her attention to her perfectly manicured other hand. "They would hang them. Draw and quarter them. Or behead them." She looks up at me, her eyes narrowing even further until I can barely see her dark blue eyes anymore. "But women, they were burned at the stake."

Sienna's voice drips with venom. Somehow, the pain of losing her brother has been channeled into a single mission: destroying me. I don't know what she'll do if she ever succeeds.

"Traitors are dishonorable. They're better off dead."

My heart climbs into my throat. I can feel Cole's gaze on me, needling me. There's so much weight in his look, so much he wants to say, but he merely sits there. Lets her tear into me.

Sienna clears her throat and resumes shuffling the note cards. It's like she's flipped a switch, and she's back to cool, collected, totally detached.

"I've changed my mind," she says, shoving some note cards in front of me. "I've decided you should be pro-*Manhattan Prep* and say it is meant as satire of the upper class. It makes more sense for the guy to think it's utter drivel."

I look through the cards. Sienna must have spent hours on these already. I swallow my pride. "Thanks."

She slaps a hand over her heart. "Was that a nicety?"

"Shut up."

"That's what I thought." She flips through the yellow cards and then pushes them onto Cole's desk.

I pick up my backpack and shove the book and note cards into it.

"I guess we're done," Sienna says.

"Oh, we're done," I say.

CHAPTER EIGHT

I turn off my car and stare out the windshield at the behemoth of a house in front of me, unable to move. Cole lives in the biggest house on Maple Falls Road, just a few houses down from Sienna.

I've been here a few times, but the elegance of it still impresses me. It's painted a beautiful muted green with gray stone accents along the front and huge rock pillars that soar up to the colossal roofline. The house must be eight thousand square feet or more, and it holds half of our school when he throws a party. I try to remember the last time I've heard gossip about his parties, and I can't seem to think of it. Which can't be right, because he used to throw parties every other month.

The front door is really two doors, both of them fourteen feet tall with lead-glass inserts. An enormous wing of garage doors stretches out to the left, while the rest of the house sprawls across manicured lawns. A big pond, complete with a waterfall, sits near the lighted front walk.

Reluctantly, I get out of my car and head to the front door to continue work on our English project. Sienna's shiny blue coupe is parked in front of one of the garage doors, like it hasn't occurred to her she could be in anyone's way.

Dread churns in my stomach. I haven't spent a second with Sienna outside of school since the funeral. The last moments of our friendship occurred just down the street. I step up onto the porch and then stop. I can hear the whisper of the Pacific. This house has a gigantic deck with a beautiful view, the best in Cedar Cove.

Unable to stall any longer, I reach up and hit the doorbell. Pretty, elegant chimes ring out inside.

Cole swings the door open, smiling as if he's happy to see me. He runs a hand through his tousled brown hair as he motions me to follow him into the house. He's wearing a thick, emerald green sweater and loose blue jeans. He's not wearing shoes or even socks, and something about that feels surprisingly intimate.

The entryway is soaring, probably thirty feet tall. A chandelier dripping with crystals hangs high overhead and pristine, polished hardwood floors, inlaid with intricate designs, head in every direction.

I follow Cole around a corner and into an enormous industrial-size kitchen, with dozens of cherry cabinets and granite countertops. Beyond it, floor-to-ceiling windows cover an expanse of at least thirty or forty feet. And then there's the view. Cole's house is perched on a knoll overlooking the rolling sand dunes and the living, breathing ocean. It looks so close I could reach out and touch it. The breaking waves are a couple hundred yards away, nothing more.

This is going to be hard. The sun sets in ten minutes. And as soon as it does, the sea may as well be calling my name—screaming it straight into my ear. We're going to have to get through all of this quickly.

I turn away from the shore and back to the kitchen. Sienna is sitting at one end of the big center island, twisting a strand of hair around her pen.

She looks up and gives me a hard look, as if she's waiting for me to insult her. But I can't muster the words. She rolls her eyes when I fail to come up with anything to say and looks back down at her notes.

"Do you want something to drink? A soda or bottle of water or anything?" Cole asks.

I shake my head and sit down on a stool, the furthest one from Sienna. Cole sits between us. I dig my bent note cards out of my pocket and pile them in front of me. Cole's are already sitting on the countertop, perfectly flat.

Sienna scowls. "You better not lose any of those. I worked really hard on them."

"Whatever," I say.

She pauses a second, like she wants to fire back, but then she just rolls her eyes. "Okay, so, thanks to that stupid fire drill, we're out of time. If we don't figure this out tonight, we're screwed." She gives me a long, lingering look, like *I'm* responsible for a stupid fire drill. Like I wanted to spend twenty-five minutes standing in the parking lot this afternoon while the fire crew figured out that some genius pulled the fire alarm as a prank and there was no fire at all.

"As moderator, I figure I'll introduce the book," Sienna says, holding a pink pen in her hand. There's a page of loopy, girlie handwriting in front of her. "I'll talk about the history of it, the popularity, the television show, et cetera, leading into the diverging commentary from both sides: those who see it as trash, diluting the quality of our literature, and those who see it as a satirical portrayal of the upper class." She flips a page in her notebook. God save us, there's another whole page filled with her writing. "The introduction should take three or four minutes, and then we'll start the actual debate."

I nod, my stomach growing heavy. I know without turning around that the sun is little more than a sliver on the horizon. The light in the room has a buttery, warm quality to it.

"You guys *have* reviewed your note cards, right?"

"Yes, *Sienna*." I want to remind her that up until Steven died, *I* was her only competition for valedictorian. After that night, I spent two weeks away from school, and I made no attempt to make up the homework. I got B's that quarter. The only time I've ever had less than a 4.0. That one blemish is enough to keep me a step behind Sienna's flawless record.

It should have been her, falling apart when he died. And yet instead, it turned into fuel. Instead of melting down, she became empty and mechanical. "Excellent. So, you're going first since your standpoint is positive, and then Cole will obliterate your argument. . . ."

Sienna keeps talking, but her voice becomes little more than a hum in my ears. The sun has set, and it feels as if invisible lines have been lashed around me, as if the ocean is reeling me in. This is the closest I've been to the ocean at dusk in two years. I clench my hands in my lap and impatiently tap my feet against the hardwood floors, eager to give into the urge to leave this place and walk across the dunes.

My irritation grows as Sienna drones on. This is a debate, not rocket science. I grit my teeth and force myself to listen to her. But try as I might to ignore the sea, it's nearly impossible. It's like the tide is actually lapping at my back, begging me to turn around.

It takes us another ten excruciating minutes to run through how the debate will work. With each passing moment, everything inside me coils tighter. And then, finally, we're done.

I stifle the urge to run full-speed out of the house and into my car.

Cole walks Sienna and me to the door, and I taste the freedom, can almost feel the water of my lake washing over my skin. We step across the threshold and part ways, not bothering to say good-bye to each other. I'm just sitting down in my seat when Sienna's tires squeal and she rips out of the driveway, disappearing through the iron gates. I guess I wasn't the only one ready to go.

I shiver against the cold as I turn the key. But then . . . nothing. Instead of the car sputtering to life, all I hear is a series of clicks. A lump forms in my throat in an instant.

No, please, this can't happen. . . .

I close my eyes and turn the key again, holding my breath, but still, the car refuses to start.

Seriously, this can't be happening. I have to get up into the mountains. I have to get to my lake. I have to swim.

Tears spring forward and I can't stop them. If I can't get to the lake . . . if I can't swim, and it gets worse and worse . . . would I buckle? Would I swim in the ocean?

No, no, that won't happen. I won't let it. I'll get the car fixed if I have to sell a kidney to do it.

But no matter what I tell myself, panic swells in my chest. The tears come faster and faster. They spill over my eyes and trail down my cheeks, dropping off at my chin. I put both hands on the wheel and bury my face in my arms. My body racks with the sobs, shakes with them,

I can't breathe. I can't think.

A tapping on the window makes me jump, and I look up to see Cole standing there. I can't make out his expression through the tears.

"Go away," I say, my voice bloated and raspy.

He tries the door, but it's locked. I close my eyes and try to wipe the tears away, hoping that by the time I open them, he'll have just disappeared.

For a second, I think I got my wish, because he stops tapping on the window. But then I hear the passenger door squeak open, and I hear him slide into the seat beside me.

I close my eyes tighter. "Please, just go away," I say. Why is he here? Why, after two years, does he give a damn?

I feel his hand on my arm and I jerk away. I don't deserve comfort. Not after what I did. Or could do again.

Cole tries again, placing his hand on my shoulder. This time I don't pull away. The heat of his fingertips burns through my jacket. It's been so long since anyone has touched me. The weight of his hand feels like a thousand pounds; it's so unnatural and unfamiliar. But it's a good weight.

"Are you okay?"

I raise my head and glare at him, then try to wipe the tears that still brim in my eyes. "Do I *look* okay to you?"

"You haven't looked okay since Steven died."

I turn away again and rest my forehead on the steering wheel. I can't believe he just said that, so simply. No one ever cares if *I'm* okay. "Everyone thinks I killed him."

"I don't."

For some reason his admission just makes the tears come anew. I purse my eyes tightly, willing them to stop, to disappear. "Why?"

"Because I saw the way you looked at him. You would have done anything to save him."

For a second, I let the tears fall without wiping them away. I take in deep, unsteady breaths, my eyes shut, concentrating on the feeling of his hand on my shoulder.

It seems as if eternity passes in silence, with Cole's steady, unwavering presence beside me. None of them know how much they hurt me, but now *he* does. I turn away from him, finally getting myself under control. Thanks to the fogged-over windows, it now feels like we're the only two souls left on earth.

"So . . . has it just been one of those days, or what? You're not the type to break down like this."

I swallow and turn back to him. I don't have the energy required to guard my emotions right now; I just look right into his hazel eyes—more green than brown—and try to keep my lips from quivering all over again.

I . . . I just . . ." I choke back the words I want to say, the words that would surely pour out if only I uncorked them. "I can't afford to fix it, and my grandmother doesn't have a car so I drive us everywhere and . . ." I let my voice trail off, because I sound pathetic to be so worked up about a car.

He stares at me for a long, pointed moment. He doesn't believe me, and I know he wants to say so. "Maybe I can fix it," he says, his voice soft. "I'm not the mechanic Steven was, but I helped him enough to pick up a thing or two."

I blink rapidly, keeping the tears from swallowing me whole all over again. "Thank you."

Cole sighs. The sound stretches out and lingers there. "All right. I'll open the garage door and we can push it inside."

I nod and look at him again, grateful he isn't pushing for something I can't give. "Thank you."

He nods, his eyes still on mine. Then he pulls away and climbs out of the car, taking all of the air with him as he shuts the door.

I stop myself from calling out after him. Two years of not talking to anyone, and now everything wants to burst out at the first possible chance. But I can't tell him the truth. I can't be that person. I can't invite him in.

I wipe the fog off the window and watch as Cole punches a series of numbers into a keypad. The door slides up, and he jogs back over to me, motions for me to unroll the window. "Put it in neutral and I'll push you over there."

I nod and do as he says. A moment later, I'm rolling into the garage. I should look ghastly in the bright lights, my eyes like sandpaper, my nose still sniffly. But I know the truth. I know I probably look just as pretty as ever. The curse of being a siren means I will always be beautiful. Even when I don't feel it.

Cole shouts at me to pop the hood, so I reach down and hit the lever. It takes him only a second to unhook the latch and get it open. "Go ahead and turn the key," he says.

I twist the key in the ignition, and just like before, I hear nothing but clicks.

I can't see Cole, but he's moving around, looking at things. "Okay, that's good."

I let go of the key and it's silent once again.

He comes around to my side of the car, wiping his hands on a paper towel. I roll down the window but don't get out. Somehow, having the door between us makes it feel safer. He looks at me with soft, concerned eyes, as if I'm fragile. "I think it might be the battery. Did you leave the lights on?"

I shake my head.

"Why don't you leave it here, and I'll drop you off at home? I can try and figure out what it is."

The panic grows inside my chest. It's instantaneous, like a dozen balloons trying to expand inside my lungs. "No, I can't. I *need* my car. You don't understand—"

"Hey. Calm down, okay?"

His voice, so soothing, makes me choke down the hysteria. He rests one hand on the windowsill and fishes a set of keys out of his jeans with the other. "Why don't you take my car, and I'll see if I can't get yours fixed? We can swap them back tomorrow."

I stare at the keys dangling in front of me. "I can't take *your* car. It's worth more than—"

"Take it," he says, jingling them again.

I should say no. I should tell him that I'll stay here and help him fix my car. But if I stay, we'll talk, and talking can lead to me telling him things. Whatever happens, the important thing is to avoid being tempted by the nearby ocean.

If I take his car, I can at least swim tonight. That will buy me one more day before the agony sets in.

I reach out and take the keys, slipping my finger into the key ring. "Are you sure?"

He nods. "Not a big deal."

I stare at the keys for a long moment. "Why are you being so nice to me?" I look up at him, and the fluorescent lights in the garage seem to be making a halo around his head.

"Because I know you didn't . . ." He swallows. "I know you didn't kill him."

My heart twists in my chest, the hollowness growing. I have the overwhelming urge to tell him he's wrong. I did kill Steven.

I get out of the car and follow him to the other end of the garage, until we're standing in front of his shiny SUV. "Just be nice to her, okay?"

And then before I can stop him, he wraps his arms around me, and we're hugging. I stiffen for a moment but then give in to the temptation and rest my cheek against his shoulder, letting him hold me as I breathe in the warm, masculine scent. He smells like the woods, like one of the big cedars or a Christmas tree. "Get some rest," he whispers.

I climb into the car and back out into the darkness. He clicks the door shut. I'm frozen for a long moment, staring at him. Just before he disappears, he gives me a wave. By the time I finally wave back, the door is already shut.

I shift into gear and leave him behind, rolling down the smooth drive. When I get to the end of his street, I turn right, heading for the mountains.

CHAPTER NINE

By the time I'm standing in the student parking lot the next morning, it's as if I've been turned inside out. My fingers ache from the icy water I used to hose off Cole's Range Rover, and my stomach just can't stop churning, despite the fact that I spent all night swimming.

I should feel refreshed and exhilarated and ready. But I feel like hell, like I haven't swam in a week. I tell myself it's because I'm worried Cole could show up and tell me that my car is dead forever, but I know that's not it.

I can't stop thinking about him. About the way he looked at me when he saw me cry. About him believing in my innocence. Even though I don't deserve it, there's something comforting about it.

It felt so good, for once, to let someone else be the strong one.

What would he do if he knew the real truth? I have to come up with something. Some way to push him away so that he never finds out what really happened, so that he never gets hurt.

I'm staring at the still dripping SUV when a familiar sound reaches my ears: my car, with its rumbling, broken exhaust. I whirl around and see Cole driving up the street. My Toyota sounds good as new. Well, as good as it's ever been, which isn't saying much.

He pulls in and kills the engine, then throws the door open. It lets loose with its usual screech. Any effort to fire off something antagonistic is immediately silenced by the sight of him. I used to think he was arrogant, but when I look at him now, all I see is pure confidence.

"You fixed it," I say.

I have my car back. My life—and the life of any guy close to the ocean—aren't at risk. It's hard not to sigh aloud.

He smiles and the dimple appears again. It still seems out of place—something lighthearted on such an intense face. "Your battery terminals had a bunch of corrosion. I just used some wire brushes to get it off. That, and baking soda. Worked like a charm."

I hold my hand out, palm up, to give him the keys. When he grabs them, his fingers brush against my skin.

Then he turns and looks at his SUV. "You washed my car?"

Oh. I thought it would be dry by the time he got here. "Um, no, there was a sprinkler on in the neighbor's yard this morning."

He snorts. "What a waste."

"Yeah, they're automatic, or something."

He shrugs and tosses me my keys. He seems . . . lighter today, like someone lifted the weight off his shoulders. I don't know what that means. "Walk you to class?"

No.

"Actually, I need to grab some stuff out of my car," I say, turning toward it. "Thanks for helping me out. I'll see you in sixth period."

But he ignores my dismissal. "No problem. I'll wait."

Awesome. Because there's nothing in my car that I need. I open the driver-side door and start digging around, looking for something, anything, worth grabbing, so he doesn't see right through me. I find a pen and shove it in my backpack and then get out of my car and follow him to the sidewalk.

We walk beside each other for a long silent moment, and I hold on to my backpack straps as if they'll keep everything from blowing away.

"Are you . . . okay?" he asks. He's looking at me, but I don't meet his gaze, I just stare straight ahead. The school doors are less than a hundred yards. A hundred yards, and I can ditch him and figure out a real plan for getting everything back under control.

I purse my lips and nod.

"You sure? Because last night . . ."

"I'm fine," I snap. I knew he'd do this. I need to fix this somehow, rewind time, and put the wall back between us.

We reach the building, and Cole pulls the door open for me. I brush by him as if the gesture is meaningless. But the truth is, it isn't; most people slam the door in my face.

Something swells inside me. A mix of somethings: hope, guilt, despair. For the first time in a long time, I am dreading pushing someone away, and I haven't even done it yet. "Thanks for your help," I say, retreating into the crowd before Cole can say anything else. I rush away, glancing back once to see if he's watching me.

Just as I turn forward again, I smash right into something hard, and my backpack crashes to the floor.

"Oh, God, I'm sorry, I wasn't looking—"

I glance up to realize it's Erik, the new guy from my English class. He reaches down to pick up my backpack and then hands it to me, meeting my gaze as he stands.

And just like that, he steals my breath away. His eyes are a shade of blue I've only ever seen in the mirror—my mirror. They're a shimmery, Caribbean-sea sort of blue.

"I—" I pause. "You . . . uh, thank you." What is it with me these days? I'm a total train wreck.

He smiles and it's breathtaking. "Sure. See you in English?"

I bite my lip and nod. His voice is deep, seductive. I take my backpack from his hand, blinking a few more times to see if his eyes change, but of course they don't.

How can his eyes look so much like mine?

In English, it's time for our debate. Sienna has typed up all of her notes from last night, and she's leading us up to the front, where a table and three chairs await.

I'm just glad this ends today. We can do the debate and move on. I can go back to life as it was. Maybe I can even get Mrs. Jensen to move my desk. But something needs to change. I can't spend a whole year next to Sienna and Cole. A few weeks, and Cole is already getting closer. I can't let him do that.

Sienna takes the seat in the middle, and Cole and I sit at opposite ends, staring right at each other. He smiles at me, and I turn away.

The gesture leaves me looking out at my classmates, and their hostile faces aren't much better.

So instead, I look at Sienna, who is, at the moment, all business, down to the erect way she's sitting. She holds her shoulders back and lifts her chin, as if she's the First Lady or something. She's even replaced her usual cardigan with a deep maroon blazer and a lace-embellished tank top. She could pass for a news anchor, with her platinum hair falling in perfect, blow-dried waves around her shoulders. Her pink-glossed lips part, and she begins her *Manhattan Prep* monologue, and the irony of her shiny hair and perfect manicured nails is almost enough to make me smile. I'm so distracted I miss my cue.

Sienna coughs and I realize what I've done. "Oh! Um, *Manhattan Prep* was created by a New Yorker *about* New Yorkers. . . ." I drone on and on for what seems like forever, flipping the pink note cards one after another. Finally, I reach the fifth card. "Which is why we must look beyond the surface and understand the motives of the author in order to truly understand the message."

Sienna beams as I draw to a close. Like a good little puppet, I did everything I was supposed to do.

"Very good. Rebuttal?"

Cole nods. "Sometimes, whether in literature, television, or real life, what is seen on the outside *should* be taken literally."

Wait, *what?!?* That's not what Sienna wrote. I look over at her without moving, and I see her fighting the urge to squirm. Sienna does not like surprises.

"Sometimes, what you see really is what you get. If the characters are portrayed as elitist snobs, bent only on popularity, is it not possible that's who they really are—and that trying to read between the lines is a waste of time?"

What the hell? I try to mirror Sienna's perfect posture and frozen expression, to avoid letting on that Cole's monologue isn't rehearsed.

He pauses, purses his lips, and stares right at me, as if we were the only two people in the room. Is he talking about me? What is this? I give up on copying Sienna and shift in my chair, my eyes darting to her. She's still a frozen picture of perfection.

"Sometimes, people simply want to believe things because it's easier that way. But it doesn't make it the truth."

I chew on my lip, glancing down at my next card. Should I jump in here? I turn away and stare out at the audience, my eyes sweeping over the faces of my classmates. I relax a little when I realize no one seems confused. They have no idea he's deviating from Sienna's precious script.

I pause when I see Erik, watching me intensely. Our eyes meet for a long second, and I take in that same brilliant blue hue before I turn away.

Cole clears his throat and then finally gets back on track, looking down to read the note cards. I zone out as the familiar speech gets rolling.

Why did he do that?

CHAPTER TEN

B y the time I enter Seaside Cemetery that Friday, I'm more confused than ever.

I thought I had everything under control this year. My entire plan rested solely on one thing: solitude. If no one is close to me, no one gets hurt, not even me. If I don't get wrapped up in other people's lives, no one is in danger.

And, yeah, maybe part of it is about punishing myself. I killed a boy who didn't deserve it, and I will pay for it. Forever. I just have to make it through high school. Then I can move on to college, leave this town, and go somewhere where people don't know me, don't look at me with accusation in their eyes. I won't make friends with anyone. I'll forever be alone, but that's what I deserve.

I sigh as reality hits me. There are so many holes in my plan— it's as if I wrote it all down on Swiss cheese. I can't leave my grandmother, not with her health failing. I can't afford to pay for classes. I can't move away from my hidden lake. I can't, I can't, I can't. But the mirage in the distance—the idea of a world where my troubles disappear—is all that I cling to these days, because reality is getting harder and harder to handle.

I walk the familiar path to Steven's grave. I stick to the walkways, because if I stepped on the grass, there would be a groove worn into it by now. The turf would give away what the cement doesn't, namely the hundreds of times I've visited Steven.

I shove my hands into my pockets as a breeze picks up. The salty air reminds me of the ocean, which, in turn, reminds me that I need to be in the water in under an hour. I drop to my knees in the grass. Steven's headstone is surrounded by flowers, left behind by people on the anniversary of his death. There are mounds of them. It's like a visual representation of how many people I hurt.

"Hey, Steven." I rock back on my heels, settling in for the next ten or so minutes I'll spend with him, my only confidant.

The Hot Wheels Chevelle is gone. I wonder who took it. Probably the landscapers. They have a lot of picky rules about what you can leave at the graves, because it makes the maintenance harder. It doesn't matter. I still have mine, sitting on the windowsill in my room. I stare at it sometimes, when I'm sitting at my desk, trying to do homework.

I take in a slow breath and close my eyes. I don't know where to start. "I've been talking to Sienna lately. Not a lot . . . but more than before. I don't deserve her friendship, but I still miss her, you know? We were so close before. I guess I'm glad she hates me so much. If she didn't, it would be so tempting to try and get what we had back."

I reach down and pick up a blade of grass, twisting it around in my fingers. "It's really hard to be around her sometimes. I can't even look at her without thinking of you."

"She misses you, you know. She'd never admit it because she doesn't like to show weakness, but I know her too well to fall for the charade."

I heave a long sigh. I don't want to talk about Sienna right now. "Cole is the only one who doesn't hate me." I feel a little pang, saying his name to Steven.

I look up at the sky. The dark clouds that have been rolling in all afternoon thicken, hanging closer and closer to land. "He's different than he was when you were around. I didn't even notice at first. He used to be more like you, you know? Laughing and joking and chasing girls. He's quieter now, kind of intense."

"He keeps trying to get me to talk to him, and it's so hard to resist. I mean he looks at me, and it's like, I could tell him everything. *Everything*, Steven. What am I supposed to do with that?"

I look down at the grass again, grass that makes it look as if he's not there at all. It erases him, turns him into another piece of earth.

The landscapers must have mowed today because I can smell the grass every time the breeze picks up.

"I probably shouldn't tell you this, huh? It's not really fair. You told me your secrets, and I never had the chance to tell you mine; and now I want to tell them to *him* when it was supposed to be you. It was *always* you."

Steven's sandy hair—and light, playful eyes—are burned into my memory, where they never leave me alone. He was the sort of life of the party that everyone notices when it's gone. Everything's been quieter without him.

My eyes lose focus, and I let the blades of grass blur into one green blob. "What do I do? Should I trust Cole? Or should I just . . . I don't know, find a way to make him hate me, like everyone else? Besides, it's not fair to you if I let him in." I look up and touch the granite. "I wish you could tell me if it's okay to move on."

I hear a dull thud behind me, so unexpected that I whirl around and end up falling backward, onto my butt, almost knocking my head into the granite.

Sienna's standing there in dark blue jeans and a buttoned-up black peacoat, and the contrast between her dark clothes and pale skin is startling. She's positively ashen as she stares at me, her jaw unhinged, her eyes wide and unblinking. Her platinum hair billows out around her in the breeze.

The thud must have been her dropping a bouquet of crimson roses, because they're sitting there by her feet. Why didn't she come on the anniversary of his death, like everyone else?

She clenches her hands at her side. "You . . . you . . ."

She can't seem to speak, and I'm so thrown off I can't get my limbs to move. We just sit there, frozen, the moment stretching on for all eternity. I finally blink and scramble to my feet.

"I'm sorry. I'll go." I rush past her, and that's when she finds her voice.

"*Wait.*"

The bite in her voice makes me stop, but I don't turn around. I just stare at the willow tree beyond the path and watch as the breeze picks up the leaves. They float away from us, silently landing among the granite headstones.

"How long have you . . ." Her voice cracks. She sounds nothing like her usual self. "How often do you come here?"

I swallow. Maybe I should have just kept walking.

"Look at me," she says.

I close my eyes and seconds pass. I can't decide how to respond, so I do as she says and turn around. I see a hundred things in her eyes, but the most frightening of all is the one thing missing: hostility.

"Tell me."

I purse my lips and swallow. I could lie. I *should* lie. But the words slip out, so quietly I'm only half sure she'll hear them. "Every day."

Her eyes tear away from me, and she looks down at her black flats. Her chest is sort of heaving, as if she ran three miles to get here. She balls her hands into fists and then stares up at the dark, cloud-filled sky and lets loose with an animalistic scream. I'm so shocked she would let go of her precious control that I actually recoil.

For once, the pain is written all over her face. Pain she's hidden so well for the last two years. And I know how much of it I caused.

When she finally looks up at me again, her eyes glisten and her perfect facade is gone. Suddenly, she's the same girl I knew, the girl I left behind that day I slipped out the backdoor during my party. The only difference is that now she's a little more broken.

My lungs climb into my throat, and my heart lands at my feet.

The first tear rolls down her cheek as her bottom lip trembles. "All this time I thought you were some cold, distant *bitch*. I thought you didn't even care that he was gone. I blamed you because you were there when he died and you didn't even seem to care. But you were just—" Her voice cuts off, and she looks back at his grave. "Did you love him?"

I don't even know I'm crying until the first tear lands on my hand.

I nod.

"Damn it, Lexi! Why didn't you tell me?" She's screaming. Her air of control has completely disappeared.

"I'm sorry, okay! I thought it was easier if you just hated me!" I throw my hands up, struggling not to just scream the words like she did.

She steps closer to me, shaking her head. Every so often she opens her mouth to speak, but then she snaps it shut. Eventually, she musters up the words. "I would have understood."

I shiver.

The silence between us stretches on for so long that the clouds open up. At last, she speaks, so quietly I can hardly hear her over the pitter patter of the rain. "Can we talk about this? Get out of here and get some coffee?"

Her voice is so hopeful I want to say yes. The girl standing in front of me right now is the girl who was my best friend, the one who knew all my secrets—except one.

But that one secret is enough to keep us apart forever.

I shake my head. "I have to go. I'm sorry. For everything, I mean." I whirl around and hurry down the path, my ears straining to hear if she's following me.

But there's only the wind and the pounding of my heart.

CHAPTER ELEVEN

spend the next afternoon at the ocean, walking the beach for the first time in months. I wade in the saltwater, and wait. For what, I don't know. The sea took everything from me. Is it so wrong to hope that it might give something back? Some whisper of an answer?

The sun crosses the sky, and I know I have only two more hours, and I haven't figured anything out. I lie down on the sand, and stare up at the clouds. They're big, white, fluffy things that don't reflect my mood. It's low tide and the ocean is calm, quietly lapping away at the sandy beach. Seagulls waddle across the sand, picking at seaweed and shells that have been exposed by the ebb of the tide.

If only I could sleep, I bet I could take a nap, right here on the sand. I bet it would feel peaceful. Relaxing, maybe. It's hard to remember what it felt like, before my sixteenth, back when I used to sleep. No wonder I'm such a wreck. I close my eyes anyway, even though I know nothing will happen, and listen to the give and take of the gentle waves, broken only by occasional screeches from the birds. I wouldn't mind lying here forever, until the tide comes in and carries me away.

But then a shadow falls across me—I can tell even through my closed eyes. I pop them open.

"It's peaceful down here, right?" Cole says quietly. He's not looking at me; he's looking at the ocean.

"What are you doing here?" I ask, as if the ocean belongs to me.

It sort of does. In some of the myths, it's as if the sirens own the ocean. It's as though they're killing because you dare disturb their corner of the universe. The original sirens, in Greek mythology, were part human, part bird, given wings to search the seas for Persephone when she was abducted. They eventually gave up and settled on an island, singing their songs and luring ships to wreck upon the shores.

I know I'm not related to *those* sirens. That sounds nothing like me. And their song is supposedly about calling out to Persephone. I don't really know what I sing, but it doesn't feel like I'm calling to some long-lost Greek goddess or anything.

There are a lot of myths, a lot of stories. None of them get it perfectly right, but each of them managed to get a little piece of it. Hans Christian Andersen's *The Little Mermaid* describes the mermaid on land for the first time, and he says every step she takes is like walking on shattered glass. Just like I feel after I miss a night of swimming. The story also says mermaids are soulless, which I hope isn't true.

I have a whole notebook crammed with research, but I've never found anything that describes how I am. Nothing that describes the way I sing. It's like . . . an overwhelming loneliness that can't be contained. When I sing, it's as if I let a little piece of that go, let it float away. It soothes me in a way that nothing in the daylight ever has. But when it's over, reality screeches back, and I hate myself for needing that.

"I live right there," Cole says, pointing behind me. His words jolt me back to reality.

I sit up and twist around, then realize with a sinking heart he's right. I've lain down right in front of his house. I'd been so deep in thought I hadn't even realized I was so far away from where I'd parked my car and that there Cole's house was, tucked away on the other side of the dunes and reed grass. I must have walked for an hour.

"Oh. Right."

I start to get up, but Cole puts a hand on my shoulder, and next thing I know, he's sitting down next to me, kicking off his flip-flops and burrowing his toes in the sand.

I stifle another sigh and just stare out to the sea. Our sides are nearly touching, and if I sit very still, I can see the rise and fall of his shoulders. An odd sense of peace washes over me. There's something calming about being near him, knowing he doesn't blame me for what happened to Steven, even though I know he should.

I watch at least a dozen waves crash into the sand before he finally speaks. "I love the ocean," he says.

I nod. I'm not so sure I do. My body loves it, but truth be told, most of the time I hate the ocean, the water, everything. The silence comes back.

Cole rolls up the sleeves of his button-down, exposing his forearms. Then he reaches down and picks up a handful of sand, lets it slip through his fingers. He's not dressed for the beach. I'm surprised he even sat down in the sand. "Do you miss him?"

I watch the sand slip from his hands for a long moment. "More than anything."

"He was going to ask you to homecoming."

My stomach flips. "How do you know that?"

He smiles, picks up another handful of sand. "He told me. It was funny, really. He asked out girls all the time. But with you, it was different. He was nervous. He kept asking me if I thought you would say yes."

I stare down at the sand between my feet. "I would have. Said yes, I mean."

"I know. That's what I told him."

I chew on my lip for a second. I shouldn't want to talk to him. I shouldn't. But I do. "Why do you keep doing this?"

"Because I hate seeing you this way. I miss the girl you used to be. I miss that smile of yours."

I shift in the sand, wishing he wouldn't look at me so directly. "Do you think Sienna is going to be okay?"

He turns his attention back to the sand. "I don't know. I hope so. It's like . . . instead of dealing with losing him, she just blocks it out, so she's never really gotten over it."

I nod, swallow the lump growing in my throat. I *will not* cry in front of him again.

"Do you remember that barbeque, the summer before he died? With the croquet?"

I feel my lips curl, the tiniest ghost of a smile. "Yeah, and I was—"

"Terrible," he says.

I try to look offended.

"Oh, come on, you know you were. But Sienna and Steven were laughing so hard it didn't bother you."

I nod. "And then they started moving all the little hoops, lining them up right in front of my ball, just so we could finish the game before it got dark."

Cole gets a faraway look in his eyes, as if he can see the whole thing playing out again. "I had fun that day."

"Me too," I say, wishing I didn't sound so wistful.

He looks over at me and for a fleeting second lets his hand rest on my knee. "Let me take you out. One night where you don't worry about any of this."

I close my eyes and concentrate on the feeling of his hand on my knee, remember what it felt like when he hugged me. When he sat by my side and let me cry. And I know I can't resist him, not right now, not in this perfect moment. "Okay."

The cell phone in Cole's pocket chirps. I pull away from him, suddenly feeling sheepish.

"How about tomorrow? I can pick you up," he says.

"No. Meet me at the theater. We can see a movie." I get up, dusting the sand from my pants. "See you then," I call over my shoulder, the soles of my shoes sinking into the sand as I rush away, fear and hope churning together in equal measure. I just agreed to a date. My first formal date, ever. I always dreamed it would be Steven, but instead it's going to be Cole. What am I doing? All he had to do was *ask,* and I waved the white flag.

When I'm far enough down the coast that he won't be able to

see me, I wade into the surf, letting it lap at my calves. It's cold. Too cold to be wading. But dusk is still an hour and a half away, and I never get this far into the ocean anymore. I avoid looking at it, being around it.

Too many people died in this ocean.

Steven's not the only one. An hour down the coast, not far from our old home, is the marina where they found my mom's body. And now, despite the risks, I'm letting Cole in, inch by inch.

And the scary thing is, this time I know what could happen.

CHAPTER TWELVE

The rain has returned. It's sprinkling, darkening the sidewalks and streets. I stand under the overhang at the movie theater in town, my hands crammed into the small pockets of my fleece jacket.

I almost didn't show up. But I just . . . couldn't seem to force myself to stay home. So, here I am, wearing my best-fitting jeans and a soft cream-colored turtleneck beneath my fleece. I even left my hair down today, falling in waves around my shoulders.

When a familiar black Range Rover pulls into the lot, all sparkle and shine, my nerves begin to dissipate. To my surprise, I calm down as I see him emerge from his car. And by the time he's walking up to me, I feel my lips curl upward into a grin.

He smiles back at me and reaches out for my hand. "Ah. See, you always did have a devastating smile," he says.

My cheeks flush, and I break eye contact, looking down at the toe of my scuffed black flats. He gives my hand a squeeze, and then we walk toward the entrance, where he buys two tickets to the comedy playing on the only screen in the place. He orders a huge tub of popcorn and some M&M's and a soda, and we find a pair of seats in the darkened back corner of the theater. It's nearly empty, except an older couple toward the front and two girls on the opposite corner.

I settle into my chair near the curtained walls and lean back. Our shoulders bump as the previews roll on-screen. Cole sets the big Coke in the cup holder between us.

"Thanks for showing up," Cole says, leaning on an elbow as I sink further into my seat.

I nod. "Of course," I say, as if I hadn't even considered the idea of standing him up.

"I have to admit, I thought you'd be a no-show." He grins, and there's a tinge of nervousness to it.

I turn to him and raise an eyebrow as if I'm surprised, but I don't think he buys it. "Okay, fine. Maybe I almost stayed home."

He tips his head to the side, the faintest of smiles playing at the corners of his lips. "I'll try to pretend that doesn't kill my ego."

And then I'm grinning again. Every logical shred of me knows this will never end with a happily ever after, but I can't bring myself to acknowledge that when all I want to do is sit here forever under the heat of his gaze.

Pop music blasts from the speakers, and I tear my eyes away from Cole to see an overarching shot of the Hollywood Hills. The camera slowly zooms in on a blue convertible with a pretty blonde at the wheel, her hair flying out around her.

Cole reaches out and takes my hand. He seems so confident, and I wonder if I should be, too.

I smile again and sink even further into my chair, silencing the doubts screaming in the back of my mind. I nestle closer to him, wondering how I ever could have thought of missing this.

The movie is longer than I expected. It's past seven by the time we walk out. I picked an early showing so that I could be up at my lake in time to swim.

Cole reaches out, links his pinky with mine. It's good that he does, because I think I might float away without him to anchor me.

It's almost dusk. It's not sprinkling anymore, and the clouds have lifted a little bit, but the concrete still gleams with rain. Cole pulls me in the opposite direction of the parking lot. "Let's go for a walk."

I guess he doesn't want this evening to end either. I meet his eyes and smile. I can't remember the last time I felt this happy, this content. I'd follow him anywhere.

But I go about five steps before I realize where we're heading. The ocean. My heart plummets. It's so close to night—the sun is nearly touching the horizon. I can't possibly be anywhere near the ocean with him. I jerk to a stop, but he's still holding my pinky, so I end up sort of shuffling and tripping, until he stops, too.

"Something wrong?"

"I have to go home," I say. "I can't—I can't leave my grandmother for too long." I don't look at him. He'll know something is going on if I meet his eyes. Instead, I stare at my brown Toyota, raindrops sparkling under the streetlamp.

"Are you sure? I thought we could go for a walk on the beach. . . "

"No," I say, too loud, too short. I hate this, hate that tonight can't be a simple high school date like it would be for anyone else. I want what he is trying to give me: a beautiful date that will live forever in my heart, the closest thing I'll ever get to a real romance.

Cole narrows his eyes. "Everything okay? We don't have to . . ."

I realize I'm giving him a total panicked-animal sort of expression and try to act as if everything is okay. "I just need to go home," I say.

"No biggie. Let me walk you to your car."

I nod, and he trails me as I walk, too quickly, to the rusted-out brown Toyota. The contented feeling has been replaced with melancholy. This is my reality. Why did I think, even for a moment, that I could change it? "Thanks for the movie," I say, yanking the door open with a loud screech. I'm about to fling myself into the seat when I feel his arm on mine. I turn to face him.

For a long moment neither of us moves; he just stares right into my eyes, as if to prove that he can see the tears threatening. He *wants* me to know that I can't hide this from him.

But instead of saying anything, instead of pushing for answers I'll never give, he just leans in slowly until his lips brush against mine—a whisper of a kiss.

But it's still a kiss.

A real, beautiful, *perfect* kiss. Everything inside me turns inside out, upside down.

And then he pulls away, his lips curling ever so slightly upward as he studies my reaction.

I smile a little, blush creeping up, and slide away from him, finally dipping into the car and plopping down onto my seat. I reach over and twist the key, and the car churns to life. My heart gallops in my chest.

"See you Monday?" I ask, staring down at my hands, suddenly shy.

"Yeah. See you then."

He lets his fingers slip off the car door, then pushes it shut, and then the window is between us.

He waves, but doesn't move as I start the car and reverse out of the parking spot.

I watch Cole in my rearview mirror until I turn a corner and he's gone.

CHAPTER THIRTEEN

It's grocery day today, so I'm standing next to the passenger door of the Toyota, holding my arm out to help my grandma to her feet. Today she's wearing a blouse with some kind of bright goofy pattern that might have been cool in the '70s. Maybe the '60s.

"I got it, I got it," she says, waving me away when I offer her my arm. I reach in through the back window and grab her cane, and we shuffle to the front steps. I grab us a cart. She likes to push it, so that she doesn't have to use her cane.

She grips the handle, and we head through the second set of automatic doors. It's warm inside, and the scent of the fried chicken from the deli makes my mouth water. "How is chemistry going these days?"

"Good. We haven't gotten our grades from the last test, but I think I only missed maybe one or two questions. Easy A."

"That's good. You want to keep those grades up this year." Gram waves at someone she recognizes, a smile lighting her face. Then she turns back to me. "They're reviewing scholarship applications at this week's rotary-club meeting," she says, one gray eyebrow raised over her warm blue eyes.

I nod. If I have any hope of going to college, I need a few scholarships. Gram knows that college means leaving her behind, and yet she still wants me to apply to all these schools, even the ones across the country.

She pushes the cart into the produce section, where mounds and mounds of fruits and vegetables shine under the bright fluorescent lights. She stops next to the bananas, and I fight the urge to point out that the bunch she's grabbing are clearly overripe. Instead I just turn away and move further into the section, my grandmother and the squeaking cart trailing behind me. I pause at a big pallet of tangerines and grab a bag.

When I look up from the tangerines, I glimpse Sienna, standing next to the bagged salads. Her hair is pulled back in a surprisingly casual low ponytail, and she's got on jeans and a baby blue hoodie. She looks more relaxed than I've seen her in a long time.

Gram shuffles toward me, the wheels of her cart squeaking louder than ever. Sienna turns around and, in that moment, seems to freeze, no more certain of what she should do than I am.

We stand and stare at each other, the tangerines and a trough of potatoes stretch on between us. I grip the bag of tangerines even tighter in my hand. If Gram is paying attention, she's going to see something's not quite right between us.

Sienna takes a step away from the salads, and I think she's just going to leave, but she doesn't. She heads in my direction, and suddenly I wish I'd stuck with a glare or a scowl.

"Hey," she says. Then Sienna turns to my grandma, who is behind me. "Hi, Mrs. Wentworth," she adds.

"Sienna. So nice to see you, dear. You never come around anymore." Gram reaches one of her pale lined hands out and pats Sienna's shoulder as her eyes dart back at me. As if she wants me to leap forward, to prove that Sienna and I are still friends. "Did Lexi get around to inviting you to movie night?"

My grandma looks my way, accusingly, and I pray Sienna doesn't give me away. I'm shocked when she just smiles sweetly, as if a movie night with her ex-BFF isn't the most absurd thing she's ever heard of. "She did—what night was it, again?"

Whoa.

"How about tomorrow? We can pick up some treats with the groceries," Gram says.

"Sure! Until then, can I borrow Lexi this afternoon? I want to show her something."

Why is she doing this? I can't be friends with her again. I can't have friends at all. It's my number one rule for a reason.

"Oh, I mean, I'm—" I start to say, but my grandma looks expectantly at me, as though Sienna inviting me over is the best news she's had in a month. Maybe if going to Sienna's just for, like, a millisecond eases her stress, I should do it. And then maybe I can weasel my way out of this movie thing while I'm there.

"Okay, uh, sure. What time?"

Sienna fidgets, reaching up to play with her simple diamond pendant. Sienna never fidgets. "Three sound okay? You can just drop by for a bit. I have something of yours."

I narrow my eyes. It's been two years since I was last at her house. If she has anything of mine, it can't be important, or I'd be missing it by now. And yet I can't help but feel something shifting as we stare at each other.

I don't know if we can be friends again. But I get the feeling that she's not my enemy anymore.

CHAPTER FOURTEEN

I drive past Cole's house on my way to Sienna's, and it's almost impossible not to stop in the middle of the road and go say hello. I just want to see that dimpled smile for a minute, feel the way I relax around him. It's more than twenty-four hours since our date, but I swear I can still feel his lips brushing against mine.

But instead of giving in to my impulse, I go right past the iron gates and turn down the slope of Sienna's long, black driveway. I roll to a stop near her garage door. Her house isn't quite as large as Cole's, but it's just as pretty. The architecture is more modern, all squares and harsh angles, but it's coupled with small sections of clapboard accents and oversized windows. Sometime in the last two years, it's been repainted from a bold red to a warm blue.

I sit in my car in the driveway, gripping the wheel so hard my knuckles turn white. It only takes a second for the car to cool.

Two years since I've been in that house. The last time was the night I killed Steven.

I stand in the middle of the living room, gripping an empty beer. It's loud in here—half the school came out to party. Sienna has cranked up the hip-hop music so that she and Nikki can dance on the couch, much to the pleasure of the guys around them. Sienna has on a flirty miniskirt, the strap of a bright yellow thong poking out the top. I roll my eyes but can't keep from smiling when she catches my eye and grins.

I turn away, heading to the kitchen for a fresh beer, purposely bumping shoulders with Kristi as I walk by. "Happy birthday!" she shouts over the music. I grin and mouth thanks, rocking my hips to the beat as I walk. I can't help myself—I feel on top of the world. It's all for me.

The clock on the wall reads ten forty as I pull another beer from the ice-filled sink. I try to look out the windows as I twist the top, but the crowd obliterates the view. It's pitch-black out there anyway.

Sienna used my sixteenth birthday as an excuse to throw her biggest party yet. Streamers twist their way across the ceiling, crisscrossing to create an almost circus-tent-like feel. School started two weeks ago, and we all want to pretend it hasn't, that the summer will just keep going.

Steven walks into the room with Cole, his best friend. His back is to me for a moment as the two of them talk. A girl walks up and catches Cole's attention. She smiles and punches his arm. He laughs, and then Steven turns away, walking toward me. He's wearing board shorts and a loose-fitting T-shirt, his skin glowing with the tan he'd gotten over the long summer. He's the kind of guy who everyone notices. One of his friends reaches out, and they bump knuckles. He's spent three years on the football team. That's all it takes to be well-known at Cedar Cove High.

Steven's eyes light up when he spots me, making me feel warm all over. The last couple of months, things have been shifting between the two of us. It's like he's finally noticing me when I've been here all along. I can't stop myself from the intense hope that he might be harboring the same feelings I have for him.

"Hey," he says, stopping right in front of me. Inches away. He leans in to be heard over the music, his breath warm on my ear. "Having fun?"

I nod and take a swig of my beer. I can't think of anything witty to say, so I take another drink, and then another, and soon I've emptied the bottle. I drop it down on the counter with a hollow thunk. Even after all these years, how is it that he makes me so nervous?

Steven leans even closer as he reaches to grab a beer from the bucket behind me, and my body temperature shoots up a few more degrees. "Do you want to go up to the deck?"

I'm not sure if he spoke the words or breathed them, right into my ear. He produces two beers and hands me one, nodding his head toward the staircase. Condensation trails down the amber glass as I take it from his hand.

I follow him through the house, leaving the thumping base beat behind, along with the forty or so classmates that fill the bottom floor. As we ascend the steps, I can't stop staring at the spot where his navy-and-red board shorts meet his lower thighs. Steven leads me through a den with dark leather furniture and teak bookshelves, then onto the balcony that overlooks the ocean.

As the door slides open, desire shoots through me, like nothing I've ever felt.

But it isn't just for Steven.

It's for the ocean, too. It's in plain sight now, swelling and flowing under the dark. All I can see is the white froth against a black backdrop. A breeze, balmy for September, whips across the deck and then dies.

Tingling waves trail up and down my limbs. It's as if the ocean is right there on the deck with me, whispering in my ear, calling my name. I watch the waves, entranced. Swimming is the only thing I want.

No, it's swimming and Steven, both all at once.

I stop in the door as Steven plunks down on a wooden Adirondack chair, popping the top on his beer and taking a slow drink. When he sets the bottle on the armrest, condensation trickles down, pooling on the red cedar boards. I stare at his fingers where they grip the bottle. My gaze lingers on his arm, then moves up to his thick biceps. He's spent three years on the football team. And it shows.

The scene in front of me, him waiting with a warm smile, patting the chair beside him, is everything I've ever wanted, but for some reason it's not enough.

"Let's go swimming," I say.

He furrows his brow for a moment and glances out at the ocean. "Really?"

I nod. "Yes."

"But this party is for you."

"We won't be gone long. Twenty minutes. Just say yes." I grin then, feeling a strange wave of excitement pulse through me. "It's my birthday, which means you're not allowed to say no."

He smiles and walks to me. And as I stand there, time slows down.

He leans in closer, presses his lips against mine. And then, before I know it, he pulls away. It happens so fast I can barely react. "Well, then, birthday girl. Lead the way."

As we walk down the steps, walk through the party, I float. Steven kissed me.

Steven. Kissed me.

Steven. Kissed. Me.

We leave through the sliding door, the sounds of the party muting as he shuts it behind us. He takes my hand, and we walk over the dunes, tripping a little bit in the dark. I nearly go down, my feet twisted in the grass, but Steven's hand on my arm saves me. And we laugh, and he finds me in the darkness and kisses me again.

And now today, I am stuck sitting in Sienna's driveway, replaying the same thing over and over, staring at my white knuckles. But I can't sit here all day. I let go of my death grip on the wheel and wiggle my fingers a little bit to get the blood pumping again. Then I shove the door open. It gives its usual screech as I slam it and walk to the front stoop before I can change my mind.

Sienna swings the door open before I can even knock, which only makes me hope that she hasn't watched me sitting in front of her house for the last five minutes.

"Hey," I say.

"Hey!" I'm surprised by how bright and airy her voice is. As though this is normal for us. "You're just in time—I can't decide between peanut butter and chocolate chip." She holds up a recipe card in each hand, waving them both around. They're bent up, smudged with flour and butter all over. A weird, melancholy wave courses through me as I look at the cute little daisy on each corner. I recognize them. The stain on the peanut-butter recipe is from the dirty mixing spoon I absentmindedly set on it three summers ago. It had been the fourth cookie recipe we'd tried, and by that point, it was all we could do to get off the couch and fetch the next dozen cookies out of the oven. We ended up watching a marathon of bad reality television, completely blissed out on sugar.

I'm overcome with the desire to reclaim everything, pretend the last two years never happened, if only for the afternoon. I want to be the girl in the kitchen, gossiping and making cookies and eating more dough than makes it into the oven.

"Both," I say.

Sienna frowns. "I only have enough eggs for one batch, unless you want to go to the store with me."

"No, I mean both together. Peanut butter chocolate chip."

"Oh." She brightens. "Why didn't I think of that?"

I shrug. It feels weird to talk about cookie recipes when we have such weightier issues to deal with. There's not just an elephant in the room; there's a whole herd of them.

I kick my shoes off—I haven't forgotten her mom's no-shoes rule—and follow her through the great room and into the kitchen. It's made to look like one of those kitchens out of a quaint farmhouse, all beautiful yellowed-buttermilk cabinets and an immense sink that resembles an antique washbasin. But, unlike a true farmhouse kitchen, this one is the size of a normal house.

Maple Falls Road really is an entirely different universe than the rest of Cedar Cove.

"Where's your mom?"

"Bridge, I think. Or Squash. Something lame."

I laugh, and the sound makes Sienna look at me abruptly. Her eye shadow is brighter than normal. Pink, set off by dark, kohl-lined eyelashes. Her surprised expression makes me realize I haven't laughed in a long time.

"Melt the butter, will you? I'm going to go grab something."

I nod and set to work. It only takes me seconds to remember where everything is stored. Spoons, bowls, measuring cups. It all comes back to me. A desperate urge to get it all back—to be friends with Sienna—overwhelms me.

I was happy in this house. I was happy as her friend.

By the time I'm whipping the warm butter in a bowl, Sienna strolls out, a tiny little bag with pink-ribbon handles dangling from her fingertips.

"What is that?" I ask, trying not to show the weird little panic that bubbles to the surface.

She sets it on the counter in front of me. "Your birthday present."

I blink, staring at the cute little bag, then turn back to the bowl, whipping the butter faster and faster, even though it's ready. "My birthday was two weeks ago."

Sienna shoves the bag toward me. One of her usually perfect French-manicured nails is chipped. "This is from your sixteenth. I never got to give it to you."

"Oh." My mouth goes dry. I force my hand to stop whipping the butter, but my grip on the spoon tightens. "You kept this for two years?"

She nods.

"Why?"

She just shrugs and pushes the bag toward me again, until it's right up against the bowl. Heart in my throat, I smile at her and grab the forgotten present. Delicate—albeit a little squished—white tissue pokes out of the shiny white-and-blue polka-dot bag. I dig my hand into it—the bag is so small my fist barely fits—and pull out the tissue.

As I unfold it, my heart twists. Inside is a bracelet, handmade out of glass seed beads. Little silver seashells and sea stars dangle from it. It's held together by a tiny polished-silver clasp. It must have taken Sienna hours to make, alternating the tiny beads in blue, green, teal. . . . It's meticulous. Perfect.

I look up at Sienna, take in the bright, expectant look in her pretty blue eyes. Sparkling like this, they look just like Steven's.

This isn't just a lost birthday gift, returned to its rightful owner. This is an offer. To pick up where we left off. And even though I know it's probably the wrong decision—the last thing I should do—I smile at Sienna and murmur a thank-you. Then I slip it on to my wrist and let her fasten it.

CHAPTER FIFTEEN

At school the next day, I feel apprehensive. Everything is changing so fast. My nightly swims at the lake are the only constant. As I step through the double doors, I don't know what to expect. Three steps in, someone shoulder checks me, just a light bump, enough to startle me. Before I can glare at whoever it is, someone else glances my way—a dark-haired guy Sienna is friends with. His eyes dart down the hall, as if he doesn't want to acknowledge me. But, instead of knocking into me as he did last week, he steps away. A tingling starts at the base of my spine, rippling upward. What was with that look?

I narrow my eyes and look around. Kristi Eckly, a girl who used to take pleasure in shunning me as a show of loyalty to Sienna, smiles slightly before rushing away.

Is it possible to feel your heart beat in your stomach? Because that's how it feels right now. As if my heart is actually pulsating in my stomach, reverberating through my limbs.

But I swam last night, so I shouldn't be nauseous. No, it's not nausea, it's nervousness. Something isn't right here.

I see Nikki up ahead, and I nearly do my usual—veer out a side door. But then she nods her head at me, as if she's totally okay with my being there. I almost stumble to a stop, but somehow I manage to keep my feet shuffling along the ugly brown carpet.

I blink, several times, waiting to see if a whole new picture swims into focus. A normal one, with people glaring at me or avoiding me altogether, but blinking doesn't change things.

It's as if I'm . . . normal again. As if I'm one of my old clique, and they're okay with me. As if they don't all hate me.

I'm torn between grinning like an idiot and hiding in the bathroom. Because I want to just . . . slip it all back on like a perfect pair of jeans and go right back to the way it once was, back when I was happy. Back when I knew what it felt like to laugh so hard my sides hurt. It would be so easy to smile at the people who are looking at me right now.

But the other half of me knows I can't possibly have all that back, that I can't step one foot on a path that could lead to more death. Sienna is one thing, but the whole group? They'll invite me to parties. Ask me to hang out with them during football games. I'm scared of that. Of how much I want it.

They'll have expectations. And questions.

I shove my hands into my fleece jacket as I see Sienna approach. She's smiling at me, a wide natural smile. She saunters over in knee-high black-leather boots with a khaki skirt and maroon turtleneck, looking every inch the A-lister she is. "Hey."

I nod. "Hey."

I still haven't figured out how to treat her, if I should act like the two years of insults and anger never existed. I'm starting to remember how it feels to have her around again.

She makes a better ally than enemy.

"Did you tell people? . . ." My voice trails off because I don't know what I planned to say next. Tell people what? That she and I hung out for almost two hours without scratching each other's eyes out? That the whole reason I've been such a bitch was because I was secretly in love with her brother? That I mourned him every day, so when he died I went off the deep end?

She chews on the inside of her cheek. "I just told them . . . that we're . . . talking. And that maybe I needed a little bit of time to figure out what I think of everything."

I nod, not because I understand what the situation is, but because there's nothing else I can do. I have no idea what she's supposed to tell people or what I'm supposed to think. It's not like they cover this in some kind of class.

Too bad they don't have siren school. I'm sure if they did, Killing Your Best Friend's Brother 101 would be required.

"Oh. Uh, thanks," I say.

She smiles. "Sure. Are we still doing movie night tonight?"

I blink. My face must betray me because she leans against the lockers next to us, lowering her voice. "I know this is weird. . . . It's just . . ." She leans in closer. "It's just . . . I don't know how I'm supposed to feel about all this. I'm so angry at you sometimes, and then I think about what I've done to you for the last two years, and I think maybe you've paid enough. I don't know what I really want. But if you want to figure it out with me . . ."

I nod, clenching my jaw. I want to smile, cry, throw my arms around her, everything all at once. I force myself to remain neutral, pretend to be unaffected by Sienna's offer.

"For, like, two seconds yesterday, it felt like it used to. Before he died. Is it stupid to want that? To forget about losing my brother for once in my life? Maybe we can't be friends like before, but I feel like we should at least . . . see."

I swallow the lump in my throat, nearly choke on it. I want to tell her it's not stupid to wish we could pretend like it was two years ago. Because I want the same thing. More than anything in the world.

Maybe . . . maybe it's not impossible to have it. It could be different this time. I know what I am, what I'm capable of, now. I'll just have to be more careful. I'll make sure no one finds out what I am. Or gets hurt because of it.

I'm tired of being alone.

"So . . . movies?" She straightens, acting like the admission of weakness, of normal human confusion, never occurred.

"Yes," I say. "That'd be great."

"Awesome. I'll come over around six," she says, flipping a strand of her hair over her shoulder. She starts to turn, but I reach out a hand to stop her.

"Thank you," I say. "For . . . you know."

Her eyes soften again. She looks as if she wants to speak, but her lips stay pursed and she just nods.

I watch her walk away before I turn to my locker. I don't know if that was the right choice. As hopeful as I'm trying to be, fear still gnaws.

• • •

I'm standing in line in the cafeteria, tapping my lunch card on the counter, when I feel a hand on my back. "Hey," Cole says.

I turn and look at him, butterflies taking flight. "Hi." I look back down at my card, feel a blush creep into my cheeks.

"I saved you a seat."

I jerk back and look over at Sienna's table, where two empty seats await.

"Oh, I don't—"

"It's cool. I promise. Just come eat with us, for old time's sake."

I swallow, glancing back at the table again. I don't know if I can take this big of a step. I wanted to ease back into things, figure them out as I went along.

I hold my tray out for the lunch lady, who puts a slice of pizza on it.

Cole rests a hand on my shoulder. "Come on. I won't take no for an answer."

And then he's smiling that gorgeous smile of his, and I find myself nodding, paying for my meal, following him across the cafeteria. He takes the seat nearest Patrick, Sienna's boyfriend, and I take the one on the end. With the group . . . but not part of it.

For a long moment, no one speaks. I take a giant bite of pizza, wishing a big hole would come and swallow me up.

"So how's your grandma?" Kristi asks, staring at me from across the table.

"Good," I say.

"I haven't seen her in forever."

Over two years, I think. "She's really into embroidery. If anyone wants a custom pillowcase . . ."

Nikki and Kristi giggle, and all of the sudden, I find myself smiling back at them. "Seriously. I've been hiding at least six sets in my closet because I can't possibly use them all, but she likes making more. Still, I feel bad when she opens the linen closet and it practically explodes all over her."

"She's so cute. I can totally picture her in that recliner of hers, surrounded by like a million pillowcases," Kristi says.

"You should come over sometime," I say, before I can stop myself. "She'd love to see you again. And you know, I'm sure you'll receive a lovely custom-made parting gift."

She laughs again. "Yeah, totally."

I want to hate the optimism building inside me, but I can't bring myself to.

I want my friends back.

CHAPTER SIXTEEN

I spend two hours cleaning the house. Vacuuming the shag carpets, washing the wood-paneled walls with sweet-smelling Murphy Oil Soap, wiping down the marbled Formica counters, and scrubbing the old pink-ceramic toilets. I even scrub the shower, though obviously it's not like Sienna is going to use it.

I'm acting as if this movie night is a date night or something. I shouldn't feel the need to impress the girl who was once my best friend, who knew me better than anyone, with a clean house. But I do.

If my grandma is suspicious of my behavior, she doesn't say anything; she just sits in her recliner flipping channels, occasionally glancing at me when I walk by.

At ten to six, the heat blasting from the woodstove has turned me into a sweaty mess, so I jump in the shower. Five minutes later,

I'm throwing on a pair of jeans and a vintage T-shirt, running a brush through my hair as I walk down the hall, the freshly vacuumed shag carpet soft between my bare toes.

I hope I look okay. It's been so long since I've tried to look good, but I don't want to seem like I'm trying too hard either. I've spent two years trying to blend in to the background.

When I reach the living room, I do a double take. Sienna is already sitting on the couch, and she and Gram are laughing.

Neither of them look like themselves. Gram is bright, happy. Sienna is light, airy, chuckling, nothing like the person she's been for the last two years. Relief surges through me.

Even though I've taken a step down a path I'm not entirely sure is the correct one, I have to keep going to see what happens.

Sienna smiles, a big, genuine, sparkling smile. It makes the mask she's worn for two years seem like a distant memory. She holds up two DVDs. "I went with classic Reese Witherspoon. *Cruel Intentions* and *Legally Blonde*."

"*Cruel Intentions* is my favorite movie," I say.

"I know." She winks at me.

Oh. Right. "Let's watch that first."

Sienna hops up off the couch to put the movie in. Right on cue, my grandma stands up. "I'll leave you girls to it. I have a bit of a headache today," she says.

"Are you sure? You can stay—"

Gram waves it away, her deeply wrinkled eyes blinking rapidly. The only time she blinks like that is when she's lying. She doesn't know I can read her so easily. "Yes, I'm rather tired, so I'm just going to go to bed early today. Popcorn is in the cupboard."

I suppress the urge to smile. I give Gram a hug, and don't miss the sparkle in her eyes. Was she really that worried about me? "Thanks, Gram."

"G'night, Mrs. Wentworth," Sienna says as she picks up the remote.

"Have fun, girls," Gram says.

And then she's gone, and it's just me, Sienna, and the bright menu screen. It illuminates the living room, somehow making the whole scene feel more awkward, like there's a big spotlight beaming down on both of us.

Sienna turns to me, and it's impossible to read the range of emotions on her face. She's not wearing as much makeup as she does at school. She looks more the way she did when we were younger, before she learned the virtues of eyeliner and blush. A junior high version of Sienna, naturally beautiful and a touch more innocent.

"You know what I was thinking about today?" she asks.

"What?"

"Do you remember when you wanted that blue Gucci purse?" she asks. "We spent three weeks scouring the malls for it."

I can't help but break into a grin. "And I ended up buying that knockoff, but you told everyone in school it was real, and they believed you?"

She's smiling back at me, a totally unguarded smile, one I haven't seen for two years. It melts what's left of my apprehension. "You did the same for me with those Prada boots."

"You mean *Prado*?"

We burst out laughing. The ice between us shatters. "It's better than that *Channel* jacket you bought at a garage sale."

My eyes widen. "I didn't know Chanel only had one *n*!"

Sienna continues smiling as she leans back into the couch, sinking into the floral cushions. "I've missed hanging out with you."

"Me too. I mean, with you." I stand abruptly. "I'll go pop some popcorn," I say. "Do you want a soda?"

"Sure. Just make sure it's—"

"Diet. I know."

It's strange, how the details come back so quickly, as if the last two years never happened.

I toss the popcorn in the microwave and dig out a big plastic bowl, then fill two glasses with soda and ice. I'm back in the living room in no time, settling down at the opposite end of the couch. The popcorn bowl sits between us.

The movie starts rolling, and I mentally revisit the last time we watched this movie together. We were at Sienna's house. Fifteen, laughing nonstop, talking about boys and clothes and a million other things that I can't even remember right now but which seemed so important at the time.

"Do you remember that camping trip we went on?" Sienna asks.

"The one with Steven?" My heart leaps to my throat. That had been the weekend I'd decided I was in love with him.

We drive for two hours, past Podunk logging towns and through old mining areas. Steven is on a mission to get to the camping spot, promising us over and over that it would be worth the long drive. He's at the wheel of his mom's SUV, his buddy Craig in the passenger seat. The two of them seem so much older than Sienna and me, sitting just behind them in the backseat. They're so mature, adult-like. Whenever I'm around them, I feel like a silly kid trying too hard to impress them.

Once we pass the last town, we drive up a winding tree-lined county road. Steven pulls onto a gravel logging road edged by soaring hemlock trees.

Finally, Steven announces that we're there and parks the SUV. Sienna and I throw the doors open, practically falling out into the warm summer air. It's early August, nearly eight, the sun falling in the sky, but it's still warm. Steven rounds the back of the SUV and starts throwing our gear out onto the ground, eventually uncovering our folding chairs in the pile of stuff in the back of the car. He arranges the four chairs so that they're facing each other, and then puts the tiny folding card table between them.

"We need to get some firewood. Do you think you two can handle the tent? The instructions are in the bag."

For a second, I think he means me and Sienna. I glance at her, but she's looking at Craig. Then I realize that Steven wants me to come with him. It's Sienna and Craig who he's asking to handle the tent.

Steven claps his hands together, meeting my eyes with a mischievous smile. "Let's go find some kindling for the fire."

"Okay," I say, trying really hard not to look him in the eyes, because if I do, I know I'll blush.

He's the only guy who has that effect on me.

He slides a mag light from the loophole on his cargo pants. "But we have to go into the woods." He flashes it right into my eyes for emphasis.

I bat it away, stars freckling my vision. "Quit it," I say, but I can hardly feign annoyance. I give up and just grin.

"May I escort you, my lady?" Steven says, in a horribly bad English accent, swirling the mag light in front of him like some kind of sword.

"You may," I say, adding a faux curtsy. He grins, sticking his elbow out.

My heart hammers harder as I tuck my hand into the crook of his elbow. He leads me away from the banter of Sienna and Craig, their laughter dying as we walk into the darkness. The trees soar out around us, and what little light the moon provides dims as we walk under the canopy of the trees.

"Your birthday is coming up, right?" He glances my way, somehow looking . . . shy? I've never seen such a nervous, timid expression in his eyes.

I nod. How did he know? Does that mean something? The whole moment seems glossy, surreal, like something I made up as I was falling asleep. Me gripping Steven's arm, him pretending I mattered.

He stops abruptly. "Did you hear that?"

I freeze on the needle-covered path, immobile as I strain to hear something. A rustling? A snapping of twigs? Other than the yellow beam of Steven's flashlight, it's too dark to see anything in the trees. Somewhere behind us Sienna shrieks, but it's a playful flirty tone, not the sound of impending danger. I will my heartbeat to slow down enough that I can make out whatever Steven heard. I stand stock-still, my head tipped to the side. My dark bangs slide into my eyes.

"Boo!" Steven hollers in my ear, jerking my arm.

I jump sky-high, putting at least two feet of air between my boots and the damp ground.

By the time I regain my senses, he's doubled over, laughing as he clutches his side.

"You jerk!" I smack his arm, but I can't stop giggling.

"Ow! That was uncalled for!" He scowls at me playfully. "Here, hold this."

I take the flashlight from him, and before I can take another breath, he grabs my waist and throws me over his shoulder, spinning me around as I shriek and playfully beat on his back. Finally, he drops me back to the ground, but it's hard to let go of his shoulders.

I don't want to be apart from him.

As he slowly releases my waist, I know what I feel for him is far more than a crush. My heart spasms in my chest and seagulls flap madly in my stomach.

I stand there and stare up into his eyes for a moment too long, hoping he's going to kiss me. Instead, he clears his throat, taking the flashlight out of my hand. "Well, how about that kindling?"

I blink away the memory as I realize Sienna is waiting for an answer. "Yeah. I remember the trip."

She pulls a strand of blonde hair and twists it around her finger as she stares at her knees. "I should have known then that you liked him."

"Why?" I chew on my lip, tasting the salt and butter from the popcorn. I grab another handful and shove it in my mouth, two kernels falling into my lap.

"We all slept in one tent, remember?" She raises an eyebrow and gives me a knowing look. She gulps down a long swig of her Coke without taking her eyes off of me.

I cough, choke on a kernel of popcorn. "What? I didn't do anything with him! I swear!"

She rolls her eyes. "But I woke up in the middle of the night, and you two weren't in the tent. I could hear you whispering outside."

"Nothing happened," I say. "We just talked all night."

"*Riiiiiight*," Sienna says, one eyebrow raised.

"I swear!" But somehow I'm smiling, and so is she. I look down and pick a piece of lint off my hoodie. "It doesn't bother you? That I liked him?"

"Do you think he liked you?"

I look up at her, realize she's serious, that she wants a real answer. "Yes. I mean, I think so."

Her lips curl into the faintest of smiles. "Then, no, it doesn't bother me. I like the idea that when he . . . when he left us, that something happy, something romantic was happening."

I frown. "It never really happened though."

She shrugs. "But if he liked you, he probably thought about it a lot. Thought about *you* a lot. My brother was a world-class flirt, but if he really cared about a girl, it took him a while to work up the nerve."

My emotions rage, back and forth and up and down. Sadness for losing Steven. Happiness for sharing a conversation like this with Sienna. Despair for knowing she'll never know why he really died. Optimism about the idea that our friendship could be repaired. Fear for what could happen if we really do become friends again, and I lose her. I can't do it twice.

"What about you and Patrick? You guys have been dating, like, eighty million years."

"One year," she corrects. "And twelve days."

"He seems super into you," I say.

"You think?" She picks up a strand of hair and twists it around her finger.

"Definitely."

"What's going on with you and Cole?"

I pick up the stray kernels of popcorn that landed on my lap. "Uh, we kind of went out last weekend."

Sienna's jaw drops. "Seriously?"

I nod.

"We should do a double date or something, sometime," she says.

"It's kind of . . . early still. For me and Cole."

Sienna shrugs. "Maybe in a few weeks then."

I nod. "That would be . . . great."

And the scary thing is that it would be.

CHAPTER SEVENTEEN

After Sienna leaves, all I want to do is swim. I want the water to clear the thoughts away, to somehow make everything make sense. The whole bumpy drive up to my lake, I can feel the anticipation. Every time my car splashes through one of the deep mud puddles, it reminds me of the lake, the feeling of the water on my skin. It's building in my stomach, churning, growing, until all I want is to leap from my car and run the mile-long trail to get to the water.

I settle for a brisk walk, coupled with the occasional flying leap over downed trees and twisted, gnarled root systems. The ground is dark, moist from the evening rains. Occasional drops from the overhead fir trees hit me on the shoulders or cheeks, but I just wipe it away and keep going. Tonight, nothing will keep me from the hours of mind-numbing swimming. Not when everything in my life is changing so quickly.

By the time my lake comes into view, I'm already peeling off my clothes. It's darker than usual today; the gray clouds still cling to the skyline, blotting out the moon and the stars.

I wade into the shallows and then dive, relishing the sluice of the water over my bare skin, ignoring the bite of the cold. I surface moments later and the song bursts out, just as it always has for the past two years.

But something doesn't feel right. I blink up at the dark night sky, trying to figure out why the lake feels different tonight.

It's as though the shadows have rearranged themselves.

I whirl around, look in every direction. As I tread water, I force a few weak notes out, but they feel *off*. It's no longer like a bottle uncorked, but like a forcefully chosen melody, one I don't know the words to and can't seem to find. I tread water, my brow furrowed. The frigid water laps against my arms, my chin. This doesn't make sense.

I clench my jaw and force the song to quiet. The water feels as if it has dropped forty degrees, but I know it hasn't changed. I'm just freaking out. As the icy water slaps against my skin, the feeling of *wrongness* just won't leave. For a reason I can't quite name, I twist around to see behind me, and look into the woods.

Eyes.

Thirty feet away, under the canopy of evergreens, is a set of deep blue eyes, expressionless, staring back at me. *Familiar* eyes. I would know that vivid Caribbean blue anywhere.

Fear and shock coarse through me. It's Erik. My mouth goes so dry I could choke, and my breath comes in weird shallow rasps. Panic consumes me. I want nothing more than to flee.

How long has he been standing there, watching me from beyond the tree line? Can he see the luminescent glow of my skin from that far away?

Then it dawns on me: How has he not followed me in yet? How has he not been lured by the siren's call?

I find my voice, raspy and uncertain, and I call out to him. "What are you doing here?"

He doesn't acknowledge me, just continues to stare. And then he takes a slow step backward.

"Why are you here?" I yell. But he takes another slow step, and then another, and another, until he's disappeared into the shadows. Soon it is as if he hadn't been there at all, as if I'd imagined the whole thing, because all I see is the shadowed tree line, jet-black under the canopy of the evergreens.

But I know I didn't hallucinate.

I paddle to the shoreline and burst out of the water in seconds, grabbing at my clothes. I don't pause to put them on until I can no longer see the lake, and even then, I struggle to get my shirt over my head while running. My arms are twisted up in my shirt when I collide with something hard. I cry out as I fall. Then I right myself.

It's just a tree.

I yank my pants on but don't bother with the shoes, just grip them harder in my hands. I sprint down the trail to my car, barely breathing until I throw myself into the seat and lock the door behind me.

My chest heaves faster and faster, but I can barely get air into my lungs. It's as if there's no oxygen inside my car. I jam my key in the ignition and throw the car into gear, spraying gravel as I gun it and head back down the mountain.

It's barely ten thirty, but I can't possibly swim.

The whole way down the mountain, the image of Erik watching me keeps floating in the darkness ahead.

Like there's another one of him standing under every tree.

CHAPTER EIGHTEEN

The following day at school, I'm freaked out, totally on edge. Why did he just . . . stand there like that? How could he listen to my song and not follow me in? What am I going to do when I see him today? And has he already told everyone what a complete and total freak I am?

Those unnatural bright blue eyes just keep coming back to me. Even in the shadows, I could see them, eyes like mine, almost glowing.

By the time I reach English class, I'm exhausted, a combination of worry and pain from only swimming for mere moments last night. I'm so caught up in thinking about last night I almost don't register that the blue eyes staring at me are real. When it finally does click that the eyes staring at me aren't a figment of my imagination, I yank backward so fast my chair lets out a wild screech on the tiled floor.

Erik smiles without looking away, a tiny lift of his lips. I blink and rip my gaze away from his. He steps away from the door to our classroom and makes his way back to his usual desk, glancing over at me once more, concern replacing his smile.

Just as he's sitting down, I jerk out of my chair. My binder and English book fly off my desk and land with a loud smack on the tiled floor. "Uh, can I go to the restroom, please?" I ask, scrambling to pick up my book and binder.

Why is he acting so normal? He was at my lake last night. He knows what I am. And he's just sitting at his desk like nothing is out of the ordinary.

Mrs. Jensen raises an eyebrow at me and looks at the clock. "You couldn't have gone between classes?"

I shake my head so fast I think my brain must smack around inside my skull.

"Very well," she says, with a dismissive wave.

I rush past Erik and leave Sienna and Cole staring, bewildered, as I yank the door open and burst into the empty hall. The door swings with such force it bangs on the cinder wall and almost comes back to hit me. I dodge it and keep going.

I'm halfway down the hallway before I can breathe again.

A few weeks ago and my routine was just as steady as ever, and now I have a sort-of boyfriend, a reconciled best friend, and a mystery transfer student who saw me swimming in my secret lake.

I find a bathroom and duck inside, slamming the bolt shut. Then I sit on a toilet in one of the stalls and rest my forehead on my knees.

I stay there until the bell rings and I can go home.

• • •

To get my mind off the Erik situation, I text Cole.

What are you doing?

I sit, my toes tapping on the hardwood floor in the dining room. Gram is at the crafts night at the senior center, and the emptiness of the house is driving me crazy.

Nothing. Want to watch a movie at my house?

It's all the invitation I need. I text back, *Give me twenty minutes.*

Then I dash into the bathroom to check my hair, which is silly because being a siren means flawless beauty, whether you want it or not. I run a comb through it anyway and then brush my teeth. When I'm done, I give one last glance in the mirror, and then flip off the lights and head to Cole's house.

Fifteen minutes later, I find myself sitting on a leather couch in a theater room in his house, wondering why he took me out to see a movie when he has such an amazing setup right here. Cole is standing next to a cute little popcorn maker, filling up a little paper bag. Previews are rolling on-screen as he walks toward me, two Cokes tucked under his arm and a bag of popcorn in his hand.

He hands me the popcorn and a soda, then pulls the blanket off the back of the couch as he sits down. He covers our legs with it. The only light in the room is coming from the projector screen and a few dim sconces in the back of the cave-like space. I wish I could stay here forever, a secluded paradise, just Cole and me and no complications. No water.

Cole slides closer, until our sides are touching. I lean into him, warm and cozy beneath the blanket.

"You okay?"

I raise a brow and give him a pointed look. "You know, you ask me that at least once a day."

He cringes. "That often, huh?"

"Yeah. What gives?"

He looks away for a minute, chewing on his lip. "I guess I feel guilty for not talking to you sooner."

I tip my head at him. "Why did things change this year? Why now?"

He pops the top on his soda and takes a slow drink. Wiping his lips, he says, "I don't know. I walked into English class that first day, and I saw you resting your head on your desk. Your eyes were closed and you looked so . . . serene. Of course, then you opened your eyes and snapped right at me—"

I grin and smack his arm. He smiles, but then he gets serious again, and I realize he wasn't kidding.

"Look, you're just a little intimidating is all."

I snort. "You lie. You don't get intimidated. Least of all by girls."

"Anyone can see you have a wall bigger than the one in China. You're just kind of . . . unapproachable. It's not like someone can catch your eye and smile if you're constantly looking down at the ground. And it felt like to talk to you directly was to risk going down in flames."

I blink. I guess I never realized just how effective I've been at keeping people at arm's length.

He turns to look at me, and with how close we're sitting, our noses are just inches apart. His voice lowers. "But I guess you're worth the risk." He leans in slowly, and I close my eyes.

This time, the kiss isn't just a brush of his lips on mine; it's more.

His fingers find the back of my neck and he pulls me into him. His kiss deepens, and I stop breathing.

After a moment he pulls away, but immediately, I want him back. I take his face in my hands and pull him toward me, pressing my lips into his. I lean into the couch and pull him against me. It's nothing like the sweet, innocent kisses of before. It's raw and hungry, and I can't get enough of it. I want this. I *need* this. Two years of being alone, and now the need to feel something burns out of control.

I nip at his bottom lip and pull him closer, closer than is possible, and kiss him harder, faster, longer, until my lungs burn. More than when I've been under water for fifteen minutes. My hands roam all over his back. My fingers find his hair and tangle in his curls. I want to forget everything. I want to just *be* with him, banish the loneliness.

He pulls back a little, breathless, his chest heaving. His wide eyes catch the flashes of light from the big screen. "Wow, I . . . I didn't think . . . didn't expect . . ." He pauses to gather his thoughts. "You spent so much time pushing me away, and now . . ." He stops again, struggles with what he wants to say as he picks up my hand and stares at our interlaced fingers.

"What?"

He worries his bottom lip and then looks me directly in the eyes. "I just *really* like you."

Why does he look so confused? "And?"

He sighs and runs a hand through his dark curls, and they get a little more unruly. I struggle to keep my hands in my lap instead of reaching up to mess them up even more.

I love it when his hair is wild. He always gels it when he's around other people.

As if hearing my thoughts, he speaks up. "You know how I've been with girls. How I was when Steven was around. But that's not who I am anymore." He pauses, runs his tongue over his teeth, deep in thought. "You're not the only one who changed when he died."

I look down, suddenly embarrassed by how desperate I must have looked, totally throwing myself at him like that. Cole wraps his arm around me.

He rests his lips against my temple. "You need to figure out what you really want from this—from *us*."

I swallow, then find myself nodding, as if to agree, as if to say I want this—want to give him more than I already have.

Even though I know what we're doing right now, in the dark theater, is the first step toward disaster, I don't care anymore.

I just sink into him as he wraps his arms around me.

CHAPTER NINETEEN

After I leave Cole's house, I drive to the lake, and the anticipation is more like dread. Erik can't be there in the tree line. He just can't.

I shake my head and tighten my grip on the wheel. I was probably imagining it last time. My mind played tricks on me, imagining him there. It had been so dark.

It makes perfect sense.

Sort of.

I shut my car off and park it in its usual spot in the shadows of the big fir tree. But then I stall. I sit and stare out at the raindrops sliding down the windshield, and I wonder if I could possibly skip swimming tonight.

But I have to know if what I saw was real.

I slide out of the car and head toward my lake, walking slowly, letting my sneakers sink in the mud. The closer I get to my destination, the edgier I feel. When I step out into the clearing, the hairs on my arms stand on end, and I stop abruptly.

He's standing next to my tree, darkly silent in the shadows. Right under the limb where I normally hang my clothes.

"I'm sorry," he says, so much louder than the sounds of the surrounding forest. His tone is smooth as honey, a deep, beautiful baritone.

I stop several yards away from him, hoping the darkness is enough to conceal the fear shivering through me. "For what?"

He looks out at the lake for a long silent moment. Part of me wants to pick up and run. I can't escape the feeling that he knows something, something I don't want to know. That whatever he says next is going to change everything.

Then, finally, he answers me. "For scaring you last night . . . and then running. Until last night, I wasn't totally sure you were what I thought you were, and so I had to follow you. Then when I saw you . . . I panicked."

I take another step backward. He knew what I was . . . before he saw me swimming?

He furrows his brow. "Are you actually afraid of me?" His head tips to the side, his blond hair sliding off his forehead.

I don't answer. I just stare at him, willing my posture to relax, but I can't seem to shake off my fears.

The concern melts into awe. "You really don't know, do you?"

I fake anger, the one thing that's gotten me through these last two years. "You have five seconds to tell me what you're doing here or I leave."

He twists away from the tree to face me fully. He leans his head to the side, a crease appearing between his brows. "I'm your match."

I raise an eyebrow and try not to snort. "No, you're just some guy who transferred to my school this year who likes to stalk people in the woods."

He sighs and breaks eye contact. His voice lowers, cracks a little. A tremor of sadness wrenches through him. "All this time, I just sort of assumed you were looking for me, too. No wonder it was so hard to find you."

It's hard to fight the urge to step closer to him when he looks so vulnerable. He reminds me of me. But I didn't manage thus far by being weak. "I don't understand." I cross my arms and hope it's enough to muffle the thunderous sounds of my heart.

He takes one more step and when I look at him up close like this, I have to fight to stay where I am.

Erik's eyes really do look like mine. Is this what he meant by match?

"I'm like you. I'm . . . drawn to the water," he says.

All I can do is stare, until the silence and the questions spinning in my head are too much. How does he know what I am? I've never told anyone.

"You're a siren?" I ask.

Erik laughs, a throaty masculine sound. "No, of course not. Sirens are women. I'm a nix."

He waits for my reaction, but I just stare.

"You've got to be kidding me," he says. "You don't know what a nix is?"

I shake my head, try to ignore the fluttery feeling in my stomach.

Erik sighs and runs a hand through his blond hair. "Why don't you know any of this? No one told you?" He pauses long enough to take in the confused expression on my face. "Wow . . . I . . ." He blows out a long slow breath. "You're cursed to swim, right? A literal curse. Hundreds of years ago, there weren't many of you. A few dozen, at best, cursed by the angry, the jealous, the spiteful. For some, a gypsy curse, others, voodoo or spells."

He turns to look at me, takes in my wide eyes, and then nods. Erik knows he's right. But how does he know this stuff?

"Nixes, we've been around centuries longer," he says, motioning to the lake. "Our curse dates back to medieval times. It's a little different than yours. We're drawn to rivers, rather than just swimming. We get . . . a sense of peace from being around them." He pauses and stares at me. "Why don't you sit down?"

I shake my head. It wouldn't be a bad idea, but I can't seem to move. Finally, he pulls his jacket off, lays it on the ground beside the tree, and forcibly maneuvers me so that I'm sitting on it. Then he kneels in front of me.

"Don't freak out, okay? I'll explain it all. Just bear with me here." He pauses, checking to make sure that I'm not about to run off. Then he continues. "The original cursed nixes were vain, proud kind of guys. Normal men, not creatures of the water. They lived hundreds of years ago, and many were noblemen.

"Then there were these witches, sorcerers, voodoo women—whatever term you want to use—who would disguise themselves as beautiful women. They'd go to the balls, the parties, whatever it took to get men to notice them. They'd court these guys, wait until they men were nearly in love with them, and then they revealed themselves as the disfigured, outwardly ugly women they were."

He blinks a few times, staring off in the distance as if he can see it playing out on a reel in his head. "If they were turned away—scorned by the men who had fallen for them—they would curse the men to the same fate. To be unloved, hideous, a lonely creature who would live a life of misery."

"But there's something no one ever thought of. If you get us together, a nix and a siren . . . it can be different. The idea of our curses is that no one could ever love us—that we could never be accepted for what we are. They didn't account for the fact that if you put two . . . cursed creatures together . . . we no longer see the curse, but the people we are."

My face is numb, and all I can feel is the bark digging into my back. Erik can't be right. It sounds so simple, so straightforward when he says it. But the curse is too complicated, too impossible to fix. "That's not possible," I say, my voice more like a whisper.

"But it is. I'm your match. We can cure each other."

"How? When? Why?"

A dozen questions spin around in my head. "And if you knew this, why did you spend the last few weeks just sitting there in class?"

"I'm sorry. I just didn't know for sure if you were a siren. It's not like you advertise it. It was a little nerve-racking to realize I was right."

I swallow, my breath shallow.

"Your curse will break when you, a siren, love someone like me, a nix, and if I in turn love you. So . . . we spend some time together. See if it can become what it needs to. See if it leads us to . . . fall in love."

I shake my head. "But I don't know you." A second thought occurs to me. "Have you killed?" A chill races down my spine, and I jerk back so fast my head smacks into the tree behind me.

Erik's bright blue eyes flare wider as understanding dawns. "No, I haven't killed. Not yet. It's what's driven me to find you. I needed to find you before that happened. Before the curse sets in on my eighteenth birthday."

Me? I can stop *his* curse? I try to calm my racing heart. Keep my hands from shaking. "Eighteenth? But for me it was—"

"Your sixteenth. I know. Nixes are different. We don't sing either."

"Then how do you . . .?"

He looks away for a second. "I wish . . ." He clears his throat. "I wish it were simply singing. Nixes don't lure women into the water. We linger around rivers, can't seem to leave them behind. We . . . we . . ." He sighs and stares up at the stars. Moments of silence tick past. "We drag women into the river. Drown them by force."

My mouth goes dry. My breath comes faster and faster.

He turns to look at me, pulls my hands into his. "Please don't be afraid of me. I don't want to be this either. No more than you want to be a siren. I hate knowing what I'm capable of, and every day I'm more worried about what I could do. I need you. You're the only one who can help me avoid this terrible fate. Together . . . we can be normal."

I shake my head and inch backward, until I'm fully backed up against the tree.

"I'm sorry. . . . I'm screwing this up. Just give me a chance to explain it all to you. From the beginning. Make you understand."

I nod because it's all I can do.

His voice is husky, smooth, and calming. "A hundred and fifty years ago, they say a nix stumbled upon a siren. He saw her swim and was awed by it. But, unlike other men, he wasn't lured by her voice. Instead, he stood there, mesmerized by her song. Neither of them knew what to do, only that they were a kind of kindred spirit. They were intrigued. They spent that night together, staring at the water. He came back every night, watched her swim, and eventually, they fell in love, and then everything changed. Their curses were broken, and they were no longer slaves to their fate. The legend is that when a nix and a siren fall in love, the curse is broken."

He rakes in a slow breath. "The curses were revenge for things our ancestors did. They're meant to force us into loneliness. The idea is that no one can possibly accept us for the monsters we are. As soon as they discover the truth . . . they leave."

I swallow. He's right. The second my dad knew what my mom was, he disappeared. And he never came back.

"But the two of us together . . . why would we judge each other for it? We're willing to look beyond it. See each other for *who* we are instead of *what* we are."

I swallow. "How do you know this?"

He smiles, gets this faraway look for a moment before meeting my eyes again. "My father is a nix, and my mother a siren. If it worked for them, it could work for us.

"It's been slow and tortuous, trying to find you. Some nixes never find who they're looking for. They live their entire lives with the curse."

Erik leans in closer, his thumb lightly tracing my jawline for a whisper of a second. "Two years ago, a high school senior—a star swimmer—drowned."

Steven.

"On its own, it wasn't enough. But then I saw a photo of your mother, drowning under unusual circumstances. And I found out she had a daughter. My parents knew how important it was to find you. So they sent me here to see if I was right."

He edges closer, meeting my eyes. "And turns out I was. You're a siren. Like nixes, sirens are rare. You're probably the only one in the world even close to my age."

He pauses and crouches lower, so we're eye to eye. "You know it makes sense. By now swimming has probably become the only thing that matters, the thing the rest of your world revolves around. You have to want more from life than the card you've been dealt."

"I . . ." I swallow. "It's just weird. To hear you talk about this. About . . . what I am. I've never talked to anyone about it." I don't know what to think of all this. The idea that everything I've lived has just been turned on its head. He looks at me, at the scared look in my eyes, and steps back. The sudden distance seems to force air into my lungs, and I take a big gasp of breath.

He furrows his brow. "I'm sorry . . . I . . . must be overwhelming you. I never considered that you wouldn't know about me. About what we . . . about us."

I swallow, find myself climbing to my feet even though I don't know why. "I just . . . this is . . . a lot to take in. I don't know what to say right now."

"You don't have to say anything. Let it settle in and we can talk more tomorrow."

"I think I have a boyfriend," I say, lamely.

He purses his lips. "I understand. That's . . ." He doesn't know what to say. He clearly hadn't expected that to be my reaction. "Unfortunate," he concludes.

"Do I still need to swim tonight?"

Erik nods. "Yes. You'll have to keep swimming, for now. Until we fall in love." He clears his throat. "I'll go."

I don't know what to say. This has been the most bizarre conversation of my life. "Will you be at school tomorrow?"

He nods. "Yes. I transferred here. I was hoping . . . hoping I could be normal. Hoping *we* could be normal. Finish school together like everyone else."

I nod, but I don't know what to say. "Can we talk about this tomorrow? When it's all . . . sunken in?"

He nods. "Yeah. Of course."

"Okay. Um, see you then?" I edge toward the water, twist around so the lake is to my back and I'm staring at him.

"Yeah. Tomorrow."

He doesn't break eye contact as he edges away into the shadows. "See you then."

And then he turns and steps into the darkness. I stand on the edge of the lake for several more minutes, waiting for him to reappear. He doesn't.

Finally, I turn to the water, the only thing that never changes.

CHAPTER TWENTY

When I walk into the cafeteria the next day, I see Erik sitting at the table with Cole and Sienna. It's the first time I've ever seen him around them; he's only there because of me, because he now knows what I am. My brain sears painfully, and I nearly turn and run, but before I can, Sienna stands and waves me over.

Students stream past me on both sides, flooding the cafeteria with the buzzing of voices. But they may as well have all simultaneously disappeared. The only people who matter in this world—in *my* world—are the three sitting together at that table. Cole and Erik should not be sitting beside each other like that. They don't belong within a mile of each other.

I force my feet to move, and I somehow make my way across the room, until I'm standing at the end of the table. Patrick, Nicki, and Kristi are at the other end of the table.

"Hey," I say. I glance at each of them, swiftly. The way the boys are looking at me makes me uneasy. Like I belong to both of them.

I try to act so much more indifferently than I really feel. I glance at Erik. He smiles. "Sienna seems to be the official welcome wagon. I was behind her in the lunch line and she insisted I shouldn't eat alone."

I nod as if this were totally normal, as if Erik is just the smoking-hot new guy from our English class and not the only person who can (allegedly) save me from my curse.

"Are you going to sit?" Sienna asks.

I realize I've been standing there like a total idiot, and plunk down on the bench across from Cole and Erik. I reach for the apple on my tray and take a big bite, happy to have something to keep me from speaking.

"Erik here was just telling us that it's eighty-seven degrees in San Diego right now. Doesn't that sound dreamy?" Sienna frowns as if the mere thought of looking pale is disturbing. "My tan is already fading."

"I'm going tanning at that new place on Griffin Street after school. You should come with," Nikki says. "You, too, if you want," she says, looking at me.

"Oh, uh, no thanks. I'm cool with the white-as-a-ghost thing."

"Suit yourself."

"Well, since you're not going tanning . . ." Cole begins, setting his slice of pizza back on his paper plate. "I thought maybe we could go down to the beach. Watch the sunset. My mom has this totally lame picnic basket from, like, 1985, but I thought we could use it."

I try to act natural. I can't believe Cole just asked me out like that, in front of everyone. Maybe he really does think he's my boyfriend. That certainly makes things with Erik even more difficult. . . .

"I'd love to, but I'm totally swamped with homework. I have a big chem test tomorrow." I nod, then take a giant bite of my apple. Too late, I realize that was a terrible excuse. Nikki has the same chemistry class as me.

I glance her way, but she's too busy readjusting her cleavage to pick up on my lie.

"Oh," he says, his voice falling.

I chew faster, swallow a painfully large bite of the apple. "Let's do something this weekend. Like . . . the sun*rise*. Much prettier than the sunset."

I could handle a sunrise. By then I'd just have to time it just right, so that the sun is showing by the time we get there, but not all of the way up.

Cole lifts an eyebrow. "But it's not over the ocean. That's kind of the point."

"Have you ever actually sat on the beach when the sun is rising?" I say, scrambling.

Cole shifts in his chair. "Um, no, I guess not. Why, is it different?"

"Trust me, it's beautiful. There's a sort of mist that clings to the ocean, and it makes it feel like you're the only person in the world."

That was terrible. But I just stare at him with a dopey hopeful smile, hoping he doesn't read further into my expression.

"Wow, Lexi, you should totally write for hallmark," Sienna says, rolling her eyes.

"Shut up, Sienna," I say. But I smile when I say it. It feels pleasant and unfamiliar. A few short weeks ago I would've glared.

"Okay. Sure," Cole says. "Saturday it is."

Sienna clears her throat. "So if you're not going to do the whole cheesy-romance-novel thing with Cole on Friday night, do you guys want to come over? My parents are out of town again. Nothing huge, but there'll be a few of us. You're invited, too," Sienna says, nodding at Erik.

I blink. Sienna was quick to accept Erik into her fold. I wonder if it has something to do with the googly-eyed look Nikki is currently giving him.

"Oh, I—" I stutter reflexively.

"Absolutely," Erik says.

I bite down on my tongue. I glance at him, and he gives me an apologetic shrug. He must think he's being helpful, becoming part of the group like this, as if it will make our future love affair all that much more believable.

I give up. "Sure," I say. "I'd love to come over."

"Great," she says, brightly, continuing her recent trend of being nice to me.

Craziness.

Suddenly, someone nudges my foot, emptying all thoughts of Sienna from my head. I glance up. Both Cole and Erik are looking at me.

I swallow and slide my foot back, hoping neither of them can reach it.

Because I don't know who is playing footsie with me.

CHAPTER TWENTY-ONE

I spend the next few days wondering if I should corner Erik and force him to back off on the party—on my life, really—but I can't bring myself to do it. It doesn't seem right to make him stay home alone. Not when I've spent two years doing exactly that. He wants to be normal as much as I do, and it seems unfair to take that away, especially since he spent all that time looking for me.

And that's how I find myself driving up Sienna's driveway, nerves raging in my stomach. Her parents are out of town. Again. I wonder how often they're around these days.

Cole offered to pick me up, but I mumbled some crap about a curfew and my grandmother. I can't stay for too long—it's almost time for my nightly swim—and I couldn't risk him asking me to stay.

Despite all the lies I've heaped on, I'm feeling . . . hopeful. Wistful. I haven't gone to a party like this in two years, and I decided to make the best of it. I even pulled out my best jeans and a cute flowery top, something that actually fits me. I feel pretty. For once, my hair isn't in a ponytail. Instead, I'm wearing it in natural spirals.

I don't want to hide tonight.

In fact, I don't want to hide at all anymore. I'm scared as hell, but I can't go on like I did before.

And so here I am, ready to see if I can really have it all back.

Sienna clearly downplayed this little shindig, because her driveway is lined with cars. Cole's, Patrick's, Nikki's, and about a dozen more I vaguely recognize from the school parking lot.

The door is half open, despite the fact that it's barely fifty degrees out. A bass beat floats toward me, vibrating the ground beneath my worn-out sneakers.

Déjà vu hits. I feel that night again, the one when everything went wrong.

But I ignore the memories dancing in the back of my mind and walk inside. The sound of clacking pool balls pulls me in to the game room to my right. Sure enough, Erik is there, leaning across the table as he lines up a shot. His platinum wavy hair slides across his forehead.

He's wearing a button-down left loose at the collar, but it does nothing to hide his sculpted body. No girl in the room seems to be immune to him. I want to walk over and hand Nikki a napkin to wipe the drool off her chin.

Behind them, Cole is perched on a stool, a stick resting on his lap.

Erik jerks the pool cue forward. It hits the cue ball, and there's a loud crack as it smashes into the other balls.

Three balls drop into the pockets in rapid succession.

Cole subtly shakes his head. He's clearly losing. Chewing his lip, he looks away from the table. And that's when he spots me. His eyes light up. He passes the stick off to Nikki without looking at her as he makes his way toward me. She scowls, but I don't care. It's impossible not to smile at him.

"Hey," Cole says, giving me a quick hug. He smells amazing, like hickory and cedar. I take in a deep, relaxing breath as he pulls me closer, nestling against him as he wraps an arm around me. "You look stunning," he says.

Erik's eyes flicker when he catches sight of us, but he doesn't say anything until he's done sinking the eight ball. Guilt sears through me. It's probably not fair to hang all over Cole in front of him. He doesn't let on that he's bothered though. If anything, he seizes the challenge. "You're just in time to play me," he says.

"No thanks," I say. I don't feel entirely comfortable being around both of them at the same time. Not after lunch. "I think I'll show Cole the house."

I realize belatedly that my excuse is a lame one. Cole has been here more than I have for the last two years. Kristi and Nikki exchange a look, but Erik doesn't pick up on it.

I drag Cole out of the den. We make our way across the tiled halls and I relish the warmth of Cole's hand under mine. How did I ever live without touching him?

Somehow, we make it to the stairs. I find myself going up the same path I took with Steven two years ago—only this time, *I'm* pulling *him*. I find myself bringing him to the same den, to the same deck, until we're standing out there, staring at the not-so-distant ocean. It gleams under the almost-setting sun.

I don't know why I brought him out here. After all my fuss and homework excuses, all my efforts to avoid our spending a date at the beach, here I am, standing on the deck, staring at the ocean as the sun begins to set.

The last time I was here, I didn't know what I was. What I was doing.

Tonight is different. Tonight I know what a dangerous game I'm playing. But, I have to see, once and for all, how strong the ocean's pull is.

No matter what happens, how my test resolves itself, I won't bring him to the ocean. I won't swim in front of him.

Worst comes to worst, Erik will come to my rescue. He'll stop me from walking out of the house with Cole in hand. He won't let me repeat my mistakes.

Cole sits down in the exact same seat that Steven chose. The entire thing replays in my head, one giant loop, over and over. But that's okay. This is my chance to re-create what happened, to choose a new ending.

I move to the railing and stare out at the ocean. When I don't sit down, Cole joins me along the deck railing. He's wearing a warm-looking zippered sweater. Somehow, he steps up behind me and, with his hands in his sweater pockets, envelops me, protecting me from the gentle fall breeze. He leans in, nestling his face against my neck.

Something in me unwinds. Having him this close just feels right, as right as swimming. In that moment, it seems impossible that Erik could be my match; it's Cole who feels like he was made to fit into my world.

"You okay?" he asks. Again.

"Better than ever," I say, so quietly I'd think he couldn't hear. But he must because he leans even closer, so close that his body pushes up against me. There's no longer space between me and the railing. My backside, my legs, feel warm from his touch.

I take another deep breath, wishing there was a way to slow down the clock, wishing I could stand out here forever, in the last place I ever saw Steven's smile.

I should feel guilty, should feel eaten alive, but I can't muster the emotion whenever I'm around Cole. When he's next to me, it's like the whole terrible Steven thing never happened and I can just . . . be.

"Really?" he asks, returning to his age-old question.

"Yeah, I think so."

He rests his cheek against the curve of my neck. "Anything you want to talk about?"

I shake my head. "Nope. I just want to stand here all night."

The sun hasn't set yet, but it's about to. I twist around, so that my back is to the ocean and, with it, everything that has haunted me for so long. Cole wraps his arms around my lower back and pulls me in, so we're hip to hip, shoulder to shoulder. I reach up, interlacing my fingers behind his head, at the base of his neck, pulling him in.

I don't know what I'm supposed to do about Erik. I don't know what makes sense anymore, what I want. I kiss Cole stronger, deeper, and he responds in kind, wrapping his arms around my back. He pushes against me, until I'm pressed into the railing with the weight of both of us. I've never felt so hungry, so alive, so *desperate* to find whatever it is that I've been afraid to look for.

Again, it's Cole who pulls away, steps back just enough that I'd have to move my feet to kiss him again. He shudders the tiniest bit before taking a deep breath and looking at me, desire swirling in his eyes even as he tries to rein it in.

Eventually my heartbeat steadies, and I stop gasping, find myself again, and look away from him, blinking hard to bring the cedar decking back into focus.

"I—" I don't know what I was going to say. But as I stand there, searching for the words, something changes. I blink several times, trying to figure out what it is. It's like I was doused with cold water.

I turn around, and that's when I realize: The sun sank on the horizon. There's no sliver of light left, just bright orange clouds, streaked with purple. Something familiar wrenches through me, and I abruptly take a large step away from Cole.

The distance is equally devastating.

"I have to go," I say, refusing to get close to him again.

Cole doesn't meet my eyes. He just stares at the ocean, darkly intense. For one long, lingering moment, it's like I could tell him everything. I want to trust him with every secret; he's the only who's never judged me.

But he would, if he knew the truth. That soft, sweet look he gives me would never surface again if he knew what really happened to Steven.

My own dad disappeared once he knew. Why wouldn't Cole do the same?

He swallows slowly, the faint curve of his Adam's apple bobbing. "I wish you would let me in. I just want to know you." He steps forward, tips my chin up. "I want you to let the wall down. Just for me."

I look down, try to hide the sadness swelling inside me. But he tips my chin a little further, so that I can't evade his look.

"You can trust me," he says.

"I know," I whisper, sadness and fear coursing through me. I'm going to lose him before I really had him. I know that now. Being with him clearly isn't enough to stop the pull of the ocean. And I can never tell him the truth, which means this will never last. For the first time, I begin to wonder if Erik has a point.

"I really like you. You know that, right?" he says.

I force myself to meet his gaze, but it only lasts a moment before I tear my eyes away, because I can't take what I see in his look. I've hurt him. It's already starting.

I stumble away from him, what's left of my heart solidifying like a block of ice in my chest. It sinks into my stomach, then my knees, more like a rock than a heart. I never should have done this. Let him in. Led him to believe we'd become something. It was cruel. Stupid. Dangerous.

I can't lie to him forever.

I make my way back to the door. The very door where I stood that night with Steven when I asked him to go swimming. Maybe this is my punishment for that moment. "I'm sorry," I say, though I'm not sure it's loud enough for him to hear. "I know I'm confusing you. I'm . . . God, I don't know. But I'm sorry."

Then I twist around and rush through the door and stumble

down the steps, the same steps I took that night I held Steven's hand in mine.

But tonight there's a difference.

Tonight, I know what could happen, and I know why I'm leaving.

I'm leaving to save him.

CHAPTER TWENTY-TWO

It's as if he knew he should come to the lake. I don't know how or why, but he's standing under my tree. Erik. How did he beat me here? Did he race up here, slamming the gas pedal down as hard as I did?

He's standing there in the shadows, silent, and I walk up and shove him.

Hard.

Despite the fact that Erik outweighs me by at least seventy or eighty pounds, he flies backward and lies on the muddy shore of the lake. I stalk forward, not stopping until I'm standing over him, one foot planted on each side of his hips. "Why do you have to be right?"

I spit the words, so angry I almost choke on them.

But then I see his expression, realize none of this is his fault.

He's hurting as much as I am. He shrugs, still lying in the mud as he turns his face away from me.

"I hate you," I say, my voice breaking.

"You don't," he says simply.

I hate it even more that he's right.

I step over him and walk to the shore. My toes nearly touch the water. I want to get in and swim right now, my body craving the cool water. But it won't change anything.

I try to rein in my pain, my anger as he sits up. His sweater is covered in mud. I shouldn't have pushed him like that. What's strange is that he didn't bother fighting back; he just let me do it. It's as if he knew I needed to get rid of the fury boiling through me.

"So," I say, turning my attention to the water.

"So . . .?" he asks.

"I want to be with him. Cole," I say.

"I know." I hear the edge of pain in his voice. The pain in my chest grows. Why do I always have to hurt people?

"But . . ."

"Yes?"

"He's already asking so many questions. He's not going to stop until he knows the truth. And then when he does, he'll just leave." I pause, wincing at the way this sounds when I say it aloud. "If I don't accidently kill him first."

"I know."

"You swear you can fix this?"

My question lingers for a long moment. Finally, he finds the words. "I can't promise you that you'll fall in love with me. But I can promise that if you do . . . if we do . . ."

I interrupt him, a new idea dawning in my mind. "Why didn't one of you guys find my mom? She died for this curse. One of you could have saved her."

"Like I said before . . . you're hard to find. It's not as if you advertise what you are."

"Yeah, I get that. But why didn't she know about your existence? My curse dates back two hundred and fifty years, and none of them went looking for you guys?"

He looks up at me from where he sits, still in the mud. "I had hoped you'd be looking for me. But I suppose I'm not surprised. Sirens rarely last long enough to pass on the legend."

I jerk back and look at him.

"I'm sorry. But it's the truth. Sirens just don't seem to handle this as well as nixes. Maybe it's the difference between men and women. Maybe it's the difference between our curses. It's just very hard to find a siren who lives long enough to pass the legend down to her daughter. Nixes, on the other hand, we've passed this down for generations. We grow up knowing what is to come. What we need to do before we reach our eighteenth birthday."

"When *is* your eighteenth birthday?"

"Twenty-seven days."

I whirl around and stare at him, my jaw unhinged. "A month? Less than a month?"

He blinks and stares back at his muddy palms. "Yeah. That's why I was so desperate to find you. Because without you? I *have* no life."

When I meet his eyes, I snap my jaw shut. Hope. That's all I see there. He actually wants to be with me, wants me to realize he's right. Wants *me* to save *him* from the things he's describing.

I'm always the one to cause pain. I've never been the one to save someone from it.

"If I agree to this . . . what comes next?"

When he stands, I cringe at the mud covering his backside. He edges forward, so his shoes hit the edge of the water. He's so much taller than I am—we stand shoulder to biceps instead of shoulder to shoulder. "We spend some time together. I can't promise you this will work. But if we fall in love . . ."

A second of silence lingers there, and we stare at each other, a hundred things passing between us. He clears his throat. "If we fall in love, the curses break."

Somehow, the look in his eyes makes everything inside me unravel. I finally see him for what he is: cursed just like me. *Screwed* is more like it. He's after the same thing. He's hoping that somehow we're okay. Somehow, we can be what everyone else is.

But he's just as scared as I am that it won't work.

"So what . . . we just hang out?"

He shrugs again, those perfectly sculpted, Greek-god-size shoulders moving upward. "I guess . . . I guess we get to know each other. See if it becomes what it is supposed to."

I swallow and take a huge step into the water. Strangely though, it doesn't have its usual calming effect.

My physical need for it abates, but my nerves don't dissipate. "Okay," I say. I feel as though I'm losing something beloved and gaining something new. It's Cole for Erik—and a lifetime of possibility. "Let's try that."

"Yeah?"

"Yes. How could I go on with my life without knowing what

this is? Tomorrow, I'll tell Cole it's over. We can . . . We can try. See where this goes. See if it can be something."

His grin is so wide, it envelops his face. After the darkness of tonight, it's like the sun is beating down on me, warming me from the inside out. I want to bask in it, enjoy it forever. Maybe with Erik . . . maybe I could.

Never have to swim again? We could do anything. Be anyone. I can give up all the drama and truly focus on college. Studies. On being someone.

How can I not want to do that? How can I not try? I have to.

And yet as I accept a hug from Erik, all I feel is my betrayal.

Because I still want Cole.

CHAPTER TWENTY-THREE

The next morning, I trudge into the halls of CCH. I know I would have lost Cole eventually, but I am dreading what is to come. In 250 years, none of the sirens in my family has ever had a guy stick by her side when he knew the truth. It's not like I'm so naïve as to think that Cole would be the first.

Besides, it's not *all* about Cole. It's about everyone within a twenty-mile radius. It's about the curse and not killing anyone ever again. And it's also about having a life, a real, normal *teenager's life*. The kind of thing I've dreamt of for so long.

So, that's it. I trade one person for everything I've ever wanted.

And yet, I don't know how to tell that to the person staring back at me with the most adoring eyes I've ever seen. Every second he stares at me, I hate myself more.

"Cole . . ." My voice trails off to a pitiful whisper.

The smile dies on his face, and he stares at me with a look that says he knows that what comes next won't be good. He reaches for my hand, and all I can do is pull it away, out of his grip.

"I just think . . ." The words choke in my throat. How can I just dump him when he's the first guy in two years I've cared about? The first guy who could hold a candle to Steven? I force the words. "You're not the right guy for me. I think we should see other people." I swallow the boulder in my throat. "I think I want . . . someone . . . more into . . ." I can't even think of a suitable excuse. There is none for what I'm doing.

Cole cares about me in a way no one else ever has. He believes in me when no one else does.

But he will never be mine. And that's the only fact that matters.

"So this is what it's like," Cole says, staring at me, his expression a mix of anguish and awe.

"What?"

"Being on the wrong side of a breakup."

My lips part, but I don't know what to say.

Again, he reaches for my hand. This time I let him hold it for one long, lingering, blissful moment. Then I pull away.

"Don't do this, Lexi."

"I'm sorry," I say. It's the only truth I've spoken. "But we both knew this wouldn't work."

"That's not true! You're scared and you're running. You know that's what this is." There's an edge to his voice—a note of panic. He knows he's already lost.

"I'm sorry, Cole. This was all a mistake," I say.

"How can you say that?" he asks, his voice now gruff and angry.

I fake anger right back. "Look, just because you're used to getting what you want, doesn't mean I'm going to change my mind. So you can quit with the entitlement." The words, so much like Ice Queen Lexi, escape before I can stop them. I guess I'm still good at masking pain with anger.

When he looks at me, his eyes shine with his pain. I just hit him right where it hurts, insinuated he's still the same guy he was two years ago. If I wanted to ensure he'd never take me back, I just did it successfully. I walk away from him without a word, my resolve weakening with every step, hating myself more and more. But I did what I had to do. At least, that's what I keep telling myself.

But it doesn't change the fact that my heart has disintegrated into a million pieces, leaving a gaping hole where it used to be.

Cole isn't sitting at Sienna's table at lunch. His absence seems bigger than anything else in the room.

Erik is sitting in the same spot he's occupied for the last week, at Sienna's table. At my table. He's motioning wildly with his hands, telling some kind of story. Everyone around him hangs on his every word. Less than a month and he's got them, hook, line, and sinker. I guess it's not hard to be popular when you look like Erik does—more like a model than a teen. He's easily the hottest guy ever to sit in this cafeteria. In high school, that means one thing: the A-list.

I'm strangely grateful for that. For Erik fitting right into my old clique. It'll make everything about this easier. I can fit into my old life, and he'll fit into it with me.

I look around, trying to find Cole, but I don't see him, and I can't just stand over here, frozen. So I fake the best smile I can muster and head to their table. There's one empty seat, next to Erik, and he beams at me when I sit next to him.

For a long second, the whole table is silent. It's like I can see them rewinding, remembering the party last Friday. It's as if they're asking themselves: Wasn't she with Cole? Nikki has some weird smirk frozen on her face, something between amusement and anger, like she can't choose between the two. A blind person would have picked up on the fact that she was into Erik. I hope she doesn't get upset that I'm going to be the one with him.

Erik covers for me by launching into a new story, trying to distract everyone. I stare down at the peeling veneer on the cafeteria table and wonder how long it would take me to rip off the whole chunk.

Sienna kicks me under the table to get my attention. Once she does, she gives me this wide-eyed "What the hell is going on?" sort of look. She wants to know where Cole is, why I'm sitting with Erik. I give her a feeble shrug and try to listen to Erik's story, but as soon as I hear "incomplete" and "thirty-yard line," I realize they're talking about football. From then on, I only pretend to listen, nodding my head occasionally.

And that's when I see Cole watching us from across the cafeteria, where he's standing in line. The expression on his face is a mix of a hundred things: anger, hurt, surprise. He must know now that it's about Erik. I didn't just run away from Cole. I ran *to* Erik. I just twisted the knife a little deeper.

If only I could tell Cole what Erik is, what he represents. Then all of this wouldn't be so bad. But I can't. I can't ever tell him that *he's* the one I want but who I can't have. And no mere apology will ever be good enough.

Even still, I mouth, "I'm sorry." But either he doesn't see me or he doesn't care. He leaves the lunch line without getting any food, stalking out of the cafeteria. The door quietly clicks shut, but to me, it seems as if it slams with a bang.

He's done with me.

Erik and I go to the ocean as the sun slips toward the horizon, to a secluded place near the bluffs outside of town. At first, I didn't want to. I was afraid that same overwhelming desire I had that night with Steven would crop up. I was afraid I'd beg Erik to swim with me, would somehow convince him to get into the water.

But Erik persuaded me otherwise. It's all part of his plan to prove to me that we really can be normal together, that I might still be driven to drown regular guys, but that I can't drown *him*. And somehow here I am, my bare toes burrowing into the sand. It's cold, wet, nothing like the summer heat of just a month ago.

He brought a blanket, a beautiful worn-out handmade quilt, and we're leaning back on our elbows, watching the sun set. Nerves multiply in my stomach. I don't know what the next twenty minutes will bring, how I'm going to feel, or why Erik is sitting there, so casual and unworried.

I haven't been on the beach at sunset since Steven. If he's wrong, I don't know if I'll be able to resist dragging him into the surf like that night.

We don't speak, we just sit, a gentle salty breeze ruffling our hair as the sun slips lower and lower on the horizon, until the sea is touching the burning-red sphere.

My breath gets shallower with each passing moment as the sun completes its arc. The sounds of the waves reach a crescendo, and I can't hear anything but the whoosh of the water, in and out, my own breath matching its pace.

The desire to swim grows within me, and I sit up, twist around, and look at Erik.

"You want it, don't you?" he asks.

I nod, clench my teeth together.

"But I won't follow you. I'm not tempted by your voice. I wasn't at the lake, and I won't be now."

I just sit there, dumbly. How can he say it, so simply? How can he know what I am and not hate me for it?

Erik drapes an arm over my shoulder and pulls me into him. I bury my face into his chest and let out the longest, slowest sigh I'm capable of. My body still burns to stand and run into the surf, but for now I ignore it. I'll go to my lake later.

"Eventually, this will be over. We can sit here, and you won't even be tempted to do what I know you're thinking right now."

Tears spring forth. They drip down my cheeks before I'm even aware they've left my eyes. Erik rests his chin on top of my head and stays silent, one hand brushing softly up and down my back.

He knows what I am and he still wants me.

Everything I ever wanted, everything that was so far beyond my reach is now obtainable.

"I want to go to homecoming," I manage to gasp out, my voice garbled with tears.

"What?"

"The dance. I want to go with all of my friends. Like I would have two years ago."

He nods and squeezes me.

"And I want to play a sport. Or maybe . . . be in some kind of club."

He doesn't speak.

"And I want to go to college somewhere far away."

Erik keeps rubbing my back, listening to me rant with a soft smile on his face. I voice the dreams I never thought were possible.

When I'm done, he pushes a lock of hair away from my eyes and simply says, "You will."

CHAPTER TWENTY-FOUR

When I walk into school on Monday, I float through the halls, still a little dazed by the unexpected turn of my life. How is it that a week ago, I knew nothing of Erik, and now I owe him everything?

"Please tell me it's not about him," a voice calls over my shoulder. I spin around and see Cole leaning against the wall.

"Who?"

Cole pushes away from the cinder block and walks up to me. "Erik."

I hesitate. I don't want to hurt him any more than I have already.

"So what's the deal? Just trade one guy for another?"

"It's not like that," I say.

"I thought we had something real."

"Don't make this harder than it has to be."

He stares right at me for a long second. "Every time something goes wrong, every time life gets hard, you withdraw."

"Please, just go."

"I'm already gone. Have a nice life."

Cole turns and walks away. I'm left standing there near tears, wishing more than anything I could run after him and explain it all. But all that would do is ensure that the next time I see him walk away, it'll be forever, no going back.

If he knows what I am, he'll never talk to me again.

Just like my dad.

The next evening, Erik takes me to the boardwalk, with its indoor putt-putt golf, bumper boats, and Go Karts. He slides his cash under the window as I stand, fidgeting, beside him, excited about going on a real date, one that isn't tainted by a thick layer of secrets. The teller hands him a handful of tickets, and Erik tears off the first two. He shoves the rest in his pocket.

"Just because you're a girl, don't expect me to go easy on you," he says, grinning widely as he leads me out the big double doors and toward the chain-link fence. A small shack squats along the outer ring of the rubber-tire-lined, asphalted Go Kart track.

"Oh, please. You're going down," I say, grinning right back. I'm glad he wanted to do this tonight. I need this after the blowout with Cole.

Erik hands two tickets to a guy in a fluorescent-orange vest and then reaches over and grips my hand. His hand is so much bigger than mine that it feels lost in his as he pulls me through the gate and leads me over to the idling Go Karts.

"I'll even give you a head start," he says, pointing to the lead car, a fiery red Kart.

"Oh, no way. I take that one, and when you lose, you'll blame it on my lead position."

I don't wait for him to respond. I bound over to the orange Kart that rumbles from its second place position.

"Fine," he says. "And when I lap you, you'll have to admit defeat."

I snap the five-point harness on and tighten the straps. I wait for the little light to turn green and test the pedals with my feet, listening as the engine roars to life. I've lived in this town my whole life and have never ridden these things. It's something silly the tourists do, something the locals scoff at.

But, despite that, it still seems like the best idea I've ever heard.

The light turns green, and I slam down the gas pedal so hard I bump the back of Erik's Kart. He glances back at me, a little surprised, but I just give him a devilish smile and do it again. The attendant scowls and points at a NO BUMPING sign as I fly past him. My hair, loose again, floats out around me as I pick up speed.

Erik veers around the first series of turns, a serpentine of lefts and rights and lefts. Then he goes down a small hill and around a sharp hairpin to the left. I'm inches behind him, my hands gripping hard at the wheel, waiting for my chance. Erik glances back, and it's enough to throw his concentration off. When a sweeping, curving turn bears to the right, he takes it too wide, and I see my shot. I slam the gas to the floor, and my bumper nudges inside his.

I could slip by him. I could coast between his steel railing and the inner wall of the track. But it's just him and me on the racing surface, and I don't want to.

I want to have a little fun. So just as I reach halfway up his car, I yank hard left, and his eyes widen as the wheel jerks violently in his hands and his car starts to skid sideways.

I grin as he turns so far that he's facing me head-on. I manage to blow him a kiss as I hit the gas again and speed past him.

By the time I come around again, the attendant is standing in the track, waving his hand across his throat as if to say, "Cut it out." He flags me back into the lineup of cars, even though I only went one lap around. But it's not enough to deflate my mood. My adrenalin is raging so hard it's impossible to wipe the grin from my face as I pull to a stop, shrugging at the worker. I pretend to be apologetic, but I suspect my dopey smile counters that impression.

Erik coasts to a stop behind me, bumping me, just a little. I unsnap my harness and jump out. "You just got *owned*," I say, still grinning.

"You cheated!"

I put a hand to my heart. "You say that like it's a bad thing."

He chuckles and throws an arm over my shoulder. "You win this round, but you haven't won the war."

"What's next?"

"Putt-putt."

I look up at him, my eyes wide and innocent. "You know my uncle is a world-class golfer? He's played against Tiger Woods."

Erik's jaw goes slack. "Seriously?"

I snort. "Nope!"

He laughs, rolling his eyes at me. Then he leads me off the track, back into the big warehouse, with its overhead fluorescent lighting and saccharine-sweet pop music. A group of tourists—obvious from their sunglasses and floppy hats—gather around the front ticket booth. A few groups linger in the putt-putt area, but the first few holes are empty. I follow Erik to a long rack of golf clubs, selecting one with a neon-pink-and-black polka-dot grip. Erik grabs a longer one with a powder blue grip.

I follow him to the start of the green Astroturf, and take in the first hole. It involves a long winding strip of green carpet bordered by white-painted boards. Erik hands two tickets to a woman sitting next to an enormous trough of golf balls and picks up two of them, tossing one my way. I barely catch it in time.

"Ladies first," Erik says, gesturing to the rubber mat where I'm supposed to put the golf ball. I raise a brow and regard him skeptically, wondering if there's an advantage to going second. Then I decide it probably doesn't make a difference and trot over to the beginning of the course.

I place the ball on the small rubber mat, then stand up and study the course with fake seriousness. I lick a finger and hold it up to the air, as if checking for wind even though we're inside. Erik snickers.

I don't know why I'm being so silly, but I feel like I need this—to be utterly, stupidly goofy, to finally make up for the two years of nothing but melancholy emptiness.

Finally, I take the shot. I hit the thing so hard it ends up bounding right over the top of one of the boards, ultimately coming to a stop in the fake gravel. "Ooopsie," I say, grinning for the thousandth time.

Erik rolls his eyes even as he smiles. He has a beautiful, wide, all-encompassing smile.

He looks back at the course and chews his lip. "So… uh…what's your favorite ice-cream flavor?" he asks, bending over to place his ball on the mat.

"Huh?"

He stands up and turns to look at me. "Shouldn't we know more about each other? If we're going to try and make this work?"

I smile. "And ice-cream flavor was at the top of the list, huh?"

He shrugs. "Ice cream *is* pretty life changing." He hits the ball gently, and it rolls across the turf, knocking into one of the boards. It crosses the curve and hits another, then another, pinging back and forth until it finally rolls to a stop a few feet shy of the hole.

Huh. Maybe he *will* win this one. I walk over to the fake rocks and retrieve my errant golf ball, then line it back up at the beginning of the course. "Vanilla. With chocolate syrup. You?"

"Rocky road. Favorite color?"

I hold up my wrist, where Sienna's bracelet dangles. "Blue. Aquamarine. Teal. Anything like the ocean." I pause. "Which is stupid, because then it just reminds me of swimming. But I can't help being drawn to it anyway. It's a love-hate thing."

To take my mind off this turn in the conversation, I abruptly go back to my golf ball and give it a whack, a little gentler this time. It nearly jumps the course again, but instead just bounces hard off the boards, pinging back and forth much faster than Erik's, more like a pinball.

But then it rolls right into the hole, and I turn back to him, triumphant.

"Nicely done," he says, walking over to me. He picks up my hand and for a second I'm confused, but then I realize he's trying to get a better look at the bracelet. Goose bumps race up my arm. There's something strangely electric about his touch.

I wonder if that's because we really are meant to be together.

He lets my fingers slide through his, but just before letting go, he twists his hand and takes mine in his, so our fingers interlace. "I prefer red myself."

"Really?"

"Yes. The opposite of the water. Nothing like the curse."

"Oh." That makes more sense. But still, somehow it doesn't seem right to me.

He lets go of my hand and steps over the Astroturf, walking to where his ball still sits, a few feet shy of the hole. He plants his feet shoulder width apart and rests his club on the turf for a second as he lines up the shot. "What do you want to major in when you go to college?"

Before I can respond, he taps the ball, and it rolls gracefully toward the hole, dropping in with a quiet clack.

I shrug. "Something with science. I'm not sure exactly. I was afraid to dream big before. You?"

He leans down and fishes our golf balls out of the hole. Then he walks back over to me. "I used to think I wanted to be an engineer. Build great big buildings, create a legacy that had nothing to do with the water."

He places my golf ball in my hand, and I grip its cool, uneven surface. "And now?"

He shrugs. "I don't know. I stopped dreaming a while ago, when I started to wonder if I'd ever succeed in finding you."

My cheeks warm, and I look away, toward the next hole. It's

romantic that he spent so long looking for me. He's so sure I'm the only girl he could ever be with.

He nudges my shoulder. "So this homecoming dance . . . When is it?"

"Two and a half weeks," I say.

"And do you have a dress?"

I think of the plastic-wrapped gown hanging in my closet, then look down at my feet. "Sort of."

"Sort of?"

I nod and meet his beautiful blue eyes, so much like the pair I see in the mirror. "Yeah. I bought it . . . two years ago. Before my, uh, priorities shifted."

I've never told Erik about Steven. Oh, sure, he knows I'm the one who drowned him. But he doesn't know I was in love with him. Doesn't know how much I still mourn his loss. Someday, I'll tell him everything. Someday, he'll know what happened. But right now? I don't want to think of it or speak of him; I want to pretend I'm normal.

He steps forward, wraps his arms around my shoulders, and pulls me into his chest. I rest my cheek against his skin. I feel my troubles sliding away, just as if the water were washing it off me. It's amazing, to think that he knows my biggest secret, and yet he doesn't care. Two years, and now I don't have to hide it.

And that's when he kisses me for the first time, right there in the middle of the golf course. I don't move at first. Erik is gentle, slow, barely brushing his lips against mine. Until I lean into him and he laces his fingers behind my neck and pulls me closer, deepening the kiss for just a moment.

And then the loudspeaker in the warehouse clicks on, and the blaring voice is enough to startle me away from him.

"I . . . uh . . . I'm . . ."

I'm what?

He smiles, looks me right in my wide eyes. "I knew it could be good between us."

I nod. Good is an understatement. That was . . . amazing.

"Do you want to see where I live?" he says.

"What?" For some reason, I hadn't pictured him living anywhere. But of course, he must.

He smiles shyly. "I thought . . . I could show you. If . . . when . . . we start spending more time together, you know, to try and break the curse. . . . Well, I thought it would be nice for you to feel comfortable there."

The idea of this—of having a life with someone—makes me so happy. "Okay."

He grins and leans forward again, giving me a quick kiss on the lips.

"Come on. It's just down the street a ways."

It's at the beach. That's all I can think as I stare at it, a quaint little beach shack, so different from Cole and Sienna's oceanfront homes just a mile or so down the shore. This one looks about a thousand square feet, all adorable clapboard accents and white-trimmed windows. Even though it's a fraction of the size of Cole's house or Sienna's house, it's far more charming. It's a home. With a big cedar porch swing suspended on chains and little pots of mums lining the walk to the beach. Round, aggregate steps lead to the sand.

Confused, I look at him, still standing near his car. "You bought a beach house?"

"Rented it."

"But why? You hate the water."

"I hate rivers. My curse isn't like yours. It's tied to a river, not all bodies of water. And besides, you love the ocean, right?"

It's weird to think it, but yes. I mean, once the curse is gone . . . there's no reason to hate it. I think.

I find myself hugging him again, a smile pulling at my lips even though I don't know why. I just like being around him, not having to hide this side of me. Having someone who *gets it* for the first time. I don't have secrets like I do with everyone else.

"How did you get this place? You're only seventeen. . . ."

"My parents arranged it all."

I look up at him, surprised. For some reason, I haven't thought much about his family. But he has one, of course.

"Like I said, he's a nix and she's a siren. They want this to work as much as I do. You'll meet them, eventually."

Oh. I wonder what it's like to have two parents who know what you are, understand your struggle. I wonder what they're like. Maybe someday I'll get to talk to his mother. She knows what it's like, being a siren.

He slides open the glass door and ushers me inside. It smells fresh, like he's left the windows open all day and the salty sea air has streamed indoors. He leads me through the living room, past the quaint wicker furniture that I can only assume came with the rental, to a small back room, lit only by a lamp with a stained-glass shade.

When I see the large king-size bed under the window, I stop abruptly and stand in the doorway. "You don't think—"

"No—of course not. If you ever want to stay over, I can take the couch." He comes back to me and tilts my head up, so that I'm looking into his eyes. "Eventually, when we've broken the curse . . . you'll sleep."

"What?"

He nods. "When we've fixed this . . . when you don't have to swim anymore . . . you will sleep."

"Why?"

He shrugs. "When the curse is gone, you won't swim, and that means you need to sleep. Just as . . . regular people do."

I can hardly remember what it's like to sleep. He leans in to kiss me, and I close my eyes.

I lose myself to the kiss and to the dreams of what will be.

CHAPTER TWENTY-FIVE

"Are you sure this isn't too slutty?" I tug at the denim miniskirt and frown as I look in the mirror. The tiny skirt fails to cover most of my upper thigh.

"Are you kidding me? If you got it, flaunt it." Sienna purses her lips as she slathers on another layer of cherry gloss.

I roll my eyes. "I'm serious. This is kind of short."

"I thought you wanted to impress Erik?"

I cross my arms and look up at Sienna's reflection in the mirror. Behind us is about two dozen discarded outfits, creating a towering mound of denim and cashmere atop her bed. "I do. I guess I'm just nervous."

"I would be too if I was you." She grins and winks at me. And yet as bright as her expression is, it changes abruptly. "Can I ask you a question?"

"Sure." I twist at the bracelet on my wrist.

"Um, well, what happened with . . ."

"Cole?"

She nods.

I chew on my bottom lip. "We weren't very good together. I mean I wanted it to work, but it just didn't. At all."

She regards me with a raised brow for several long moments. I think she's going to call me on it. She tips her head to the side and opens her mouth to say something. Then she shrugs. "You do know Erik is the hottest guy at CCH in, well, ever, right? And he is totally into you."

I blush and scrunch my shoulders. "Seriously? Because I feel like I'm all over the place, a total nervous mess."

Sienna laughs. "Completely justified. That guy could melt an iceberg, he's so hot. Which is why you should trust me when I say you should definitely wear that skirt."

I chew on my lip and look in the mirror again, stare at the nervous expression in my eyes, and then take a sweeping gaze over the skin-baring outfit. "Fine, you convinced me."

"Good, because the guys are here."

My heart skips a beat. "What? When?"

"While you were in the bathroom putting that on. Let's go."

"But I'm not ready!"

"Yes you are. Trust me. Once he sees your legs, he won't be looking at anything else."

I laugh and let her pull me out the door, the buckles on the chunky brown boots she loaned me jangling as she drags me through the house.

Tonight is going to be fun. Really, truly fun. There's a fall harvest festival in town, right off Port Street. I haven't been to it in years, because it's close to the piers and the water. From the top of the Ferris wheel, it has a sweeping view of the ocean. And by the time it gets going in earnest, I'm usually up in the mountains, ensconced in my lake.

Erik and Patrick lounge on the chocolate-leather couch in the living room. Erik has one foot propped up on the opposite knee. He's got on crisp, deep indigo blue jeans and a navy V-necked sweater. A white T-shirt peeks out from underneath. His hair must have a light layer of gel, because it's out of his face for once, and it makes his blue eyes seem even brighter.

He stands and his eyes sweep over me for a second, a smile playing at the edges of his lips. "Wow. You look . . ."

I grin and hug him, take in the natural salty scent that clings to his skin. "You look pretty good yourself."

We follow Sienna and Patrick outside to where Patrick's old Bronco sits, its flawless coat of red paint gleaming. Patrick could afford a newer car, but I guess he's like Steven, into the classics. Erik opens the back door for me. I climb in and slide over to give him room. He slams the door shut, and we buckle up as Patrick throws it in reverse. In moments, we're rolling down the surface streets toward the main drag in town. The Festival always straddles the two parking lots between the grocery store and the post office, at the end of Port Street, not far from the tourist shops.

Patrick parks on a side street behind the little cinder-block post office. He seems to have found the only empty spot within several blocks. Erik squeezes my hand and then climbs out, pulling me with him.

Music floods my ears. Country or something with a fiddle. Not normally my taste, but I can't help but smile as the twangy voice of a girl blares from the speakers. I want to dance. I want to dance until the festival is over and I'm the last one standing there on the floor.

We follow Patrick and Sienna toward the festival. Flags and streamers are strung back and forth across the space, flapping in the sea breeze. Orange, yellow, and white Christmas lights are wrapped around every light pole.

Sienna, in her high heels, trips on a crack in the sidewalk and knocks into Patrick. He makes a big show of saving her. She giggles as he swoops in and picks her up, carrying her as if she broke an ankle. They pass a large garbage can, and he pretends like he's going to throw her in. She shrieks, playfully hitting him in the shoulder, until Patrick sets her back down.

The relationship glow reflects off the two of them and onto me and Erik. I grin at him, loving every moment of this. He smiles back at me, genuine happiness in his eyes as he leans down and brushes his lips against mine. I have to fight the urge to close my eyes. It's still a little strange to me that I can be myself around him—that he knows what I am and doesn't care. He's as much of a drug to me as the water is.

We pass through the festival's main entry and are assaulted by the smells: fried onions, cotton candy, freshly squeezed lemonade, grilled corn on the cob. Tufts of smoke fill the air from the barbecues, and occasional shrill ringing bursts from the games. A small roller coaster clackety-clacks up the incline. The band grows louder.

"What do you want to do first?" Sienna asks, spinning around and walking backward. Patrick holds on to her elbows to keep her from falling over on the uneven ground.

"Ferris wheel," I say.

"Done." She spins around again and skips off toward the Ferris wheel perched at the edge of the lot, the corner closest to the marina and the piers.

It's a warm night for Autumn, with a sky so cloudless I could spend all night counting the stars. A gentle briny breeze floats across the place, mingling with the scent of fried fair food and caramel apples.

The Ferris wheel is small, the sort that two people sit side by side in. Sienna and Patrick climb into the first car, with Erik and me behind them in the next one. The car rises slowly, pausing momentarily a few times to let other riders on.

The car above us starts to swing back and forth, and then Patrick's voice calls out, "If the ride is a rockin', don't come a knockin'!"

I roll my eyes as I hear Sienna chide him, but the car swings for a while longer before finally stilling. We rise higher, until we've surpassed the roller coaster and the stage. The landscape opens up around us. Erik slides an arm behind me and pulls me up against him. I lean into his chest and watch as we rise high enough to see the ocean spread out below us. It sparkles under the twinkling stars, eventually disappearing into the mist.

Our car stops at the tip-top, so that Sienna and Patrick aren't in view anymore, and it's just Erik and me, like we're the only souls on earth. The faint sounds of the band still trickle up to us, but it's a ballad now, a sweet violin solo as our only company in the darkness.

My hunger for the ocean grows, as I stare down at it.

"You want to swim, huh?"

I nod.

"If it gets unbearable, tell me. We'll go."

I nod, grateful he understands, and turn to look him in the eyes. I tip my head back, and Erik leans over me enough so that we can kiss again. This time his tongue traces my lips until I part them. And then we're kissing like that, more heated, deeper than before. Unlike the kisses with Cole, this one doesn't end too soon.

I'm so lost in the moment, I nearly jump out of my seat when someone clears their throat. I look up to see the attendant standing there, the next riders behind him.

Oh, right. We're at the bottom.

I scramble out of the car, accepting Erik's hand as he leads me around the attendant. But just as I pass him, I glance over and nearly trip over my own feet.

Cole is standing there with Nikki. Are they together now? Or are they here as friends? I blink rapidly and look past them. Kristi's here, too, with a guy I've seen her talking to at school. Are they also on a double date?

Why do I feel like my insides are in a blender right now? It's just Nikki. There's no way he'd date her. There's no way he'd get over me so quickly.

But I'm here with Erik. Cole thinks *I* got over *him* that quickly.

I tear my eyes away from him, hoping somehow to get rid of the image of Nikki's hand on Cole's arm. Of course, they would be here. Everyone goes to the Harvest Festival.

Erik notices my expression but doesn't call me on it. He attempts to distract me. "What now?" he asks. We walk past one of the games that rings out with a shrill bell, overstuffed cartoon characters dangling from the edges of the booth.

"We dance?"

"Is that a question?" He asks, turning to look at me.

"No. It's a request."

He grins, another gleaming smile. "Consider it granted."

I'm not sure where Sienna disappeared to, but I can't bring myself to care as he leads me through the crowd. We weave between stands and strollers and other kids from school too absorbed in their own conversation to notice us, until we're in the area they've set up for the band. The dance area is surrounded by straw bales and is packed with people—couples young and old.

The band seems to have gone from country to swing, and everyone is going crazy, spinning and swinging, laughing and smiling.

"Uh, do you know how to swing dance?" I ask, grimacing.

"Yes."

I spin around and look at him, wondering if he's joking. "Seriously?"

"Yep. You?"

"We covered it in PE last year, but I wasn't very good," I say, giving him an apologetic look. "Prepare to have your toes smashed."

"We'll see about that."

He pulls me into the crowd, then spins me around so fast I can hardly breathe. He takes my hands in his, our fingers interlaced and palms together. "Just put your trust in me, and everything will be fine. Can you do that?"

I nod, but I'm hardly ready when suddenly he pulls me toward him. Just as I think I'm going to crash right into his chest, stumble over his feet, he pushes me away. I nearly lose my balance, but my arm twists above my head, and I'm spinning in a circle. For a millisecond, my back is up against his chest, but then he spins me the opposite direction. Finally, he takes my spare hand, and I end up back where I started.

I burst into laughter, because I have no idea how he just did that, but I don't stop dancing. Instead, I pick up on his rhythm. I forfeit all control to Erik, allowing my body to go where he leads it. I let myself lose my balance here and there and hope he'll catch me.

And he does. We're flying all over, spinning, dipping, twisting, and I can't seem to stop grinning like a fool as I shuffle my feet this way and that, wherever he leads me. The song bleeds into the next and then the next, until I'm not even sure it's swing music anymore. But still we don't stop.

We dance for so long that I lose track of time, which seems an unbelievable feat when my hunger for the ocean grows with each tick of the clock. I wouldn't be able to do this with anyone but Erik. Knowing he won't let me walk away from him, won't let me out of sight, somehow makes it possible to relax and enjoy myself.

Finally, the beat drifts away, and a slow melody picks up. A love song, clear as day, echoes from the speakers. And only then do I let my feet slow.

Erik releases my left hand so that he can put his arm around my lower waist. He pulls me against his body, warmer than the night.

CHAPTER TWENTY-SIX

A week after the festival, Sienna's blue coupe follows Nikki's dark Mitsubishi sedan up a particularly winding part of Route 101. The sky above us is black with storm clouds. It's a particularly dangerous part of the highway. The cliffs hug the road to our left; the ocean licks at the rocks below to our right, at least fifty feet down. There won't be a real shoulder for at least another half mile.

It's unbelievably dark, and yet the sun won't set for another hour.

Erik and I are crammed in the backseat of Sienna's coupe as we follow the two cars ahead, their headlights illuminating the pavement in front of our caravan. Hip-hop blares from Sienna's speakers as Erik's hand rests on my knees. It's too loud to talk to Erik, but we smile at each other in the darkness, trusting our lives to Sienna's marginal driving skills.

Up ahead, a red blinker flashes, and taillights flare brighter. Sienna slows, turning off the road and driving through a rusted open old gate, barely hanging on by one hinge. Dilapidated wire fencing sags between old iron T posts, mostly obscured by the overgrown reedy grass that grows this close to the ocean.

Our caravan glides quietly up the gravel, winding back and forth on a few lazy switchbacks. The headlights illuminate secluded spots of the sparse grassy hillside until a wide, empty gravel lot opens up. The two cars in front of us pull up next to each other, and then Sienna does the same. "We're here," she says, glancing back at us as she turns off the radio. Patrick throws his door open and yanks his seat forward to allow us to climb out.

Outside the car, I watch as six of my classmates—Nikki included— pile out of the other cars. I am inordinately happy that Cole isn't here tonight. I haven't figured out yet if something is going on between him and Nikki. And frankly, if it is, I don't want to know.

One of the guys lets loose with a ridiculous coyote screech, his hands above his head in a rock-on kind of signal.

Erik and I follow the others to this evening's destination.

The lighthouse.

But this lighthouse isn't exactly serving its original function. It juts into the dark sky, completely black, devoid of . . . anything. It's engulfed in total blackness, has been for at least a decade.

Patrick, Brian, and Danny all switch flashlights on.

Erik leans in, whispers into my ear, "Sorry. I didn't get the memo about the flashlights."

I grin up at him in the gray of the evening light. "It's okay. I forgive you."

We manage to find each other's hands in the darkness and to interlace our fingers. Ahead, the storm clouds seem to have closed in on the lighthouse. It's as if it has disappeared right into the clouds.

We walk in silence, and soon my sneakers hit pavement. The last two hundred feet before the backdoor is a crooked, cracked old sidewalk.

"Are you guys sure this place is still unlocked?" someone asks. Nikki mutters something I can't quite make out. To my left, Kristi giggles.

I haven't been in a group like this in a while. At Sienna's, it's easy to detach from everyone, find a quiet room. But today, we're all together, all on the same mission. And in the darkness, no one separates from the pack.

Right on time, the ground rumbles with thunder. "Told you," Sienna says, throwing a look over her shoulder.

Excited whispers mount as we reach the only door to the lighthouse. Nikki stops, her hand on the knob, and glances back at all of us. Then she purses her lips and turns back to the door, twisting at the knob.

It swings open.

"Yes!" Sienna jumps up and hugs Patrick. I let out the air I'd been holding.

We file one by one through the entry, and by the time I get inside, a whole line of people are already climbing the old steel-grate steps. The stairs wind around and around in a lazy spiral, all the way to the top.

I wait in silence for a second. Then I grab the rusted wrought iron and follow my friends up, the steps groaning and creaking under our collective weight.

It must take ten minutes for our whole group to make it to the top. Beams of flashlights bounce around inside the cylindrical area as we wind around and around the spiral staircase.

And then Nikki finds another door to push, and we emerge onto the platform. It's just as dark here as it was below. The electrical system is totally shot—not only do the spotlights not work, but neither do the overhead lights.

We fan out around the windows, stare out at the ocean raging against the rocky cliffs below us. The wind has been picking up, and the sea is frothing white.

Lightning streaks across the horizon. Nikki shrieks and jerks back, away from the window. Someone laughs.

We used to come up here all the time, the whole group of us. Whenever the weather people predicted a storm, we'd all pile in a car and come up to the old abandoned lighthouse on the bluffs. Most of the time, the "storm" turned out to be nothing, a boring false alarm. But after we saw real lightning for the first time, we were all hooked. The dark magic of Mother Nature was enough to keep us coming back, over and over.

Erik and I hang back, and he pulls me closer, leans in close enough that his lips brush my earlobe. "This is amazing," he says, as the air around us crackles with a thunder boom.

I nod. "I know."

A bolt of lightning streaks across the ocean.

"I meant us," he says, his voice lower than ever.

I smile, then turn to meet his eyes.

"I know."

• • •

If it seemed like the atmosphere at school a few weeks ago had shifted, today it feels like the entire world flipped around, turned inside out.

I walk in, and Nikki smiles and waves at me. "Last night rocked," she says, rushing by. She twists around and walks backward so we can maintain eye contact. "We are so doing it again!"

I grin at her as she dashes out the door toward the gym. She has first-period PE. I know, because she's bitched about it for two weeks straight. It ruins her hair or something.

I head to my locker and am inches away when Brian, one of the guys from last night walks by. He nods at me, a happy, slightly tired smile on his face. "Last night was epic!" he says, giving me a fist bump as he passes. "Next time we're staying overnight!"

I laugh. I hope by then, my curse will be gone. Every night I go swimming, I hope it's one of the last times.

It's hard to imagine, but it could happen. I turn back to the lock, spinning it twice toward the right when I feel hands wrap around my waist. Before I can react, a warm cheek presses against my face. "So this is what it's like, huh?"

I turn at the husky voice and smile. Erik's hair is wild and loose today, and like the others, he looks a little tired but happy.

"What?"

His grin gets bigger. "Being one of them. Being normal."

I smile and nod. "Yeah. I guess so."

"Pretty awesome, huh?"

I sigh, totally content inside these four walls for the first time in a long time. "Yeah. I'd have to agree."

"And homecoming is this weekend?"

I grin. "Yeah. Saturday."

"Great. See you at lunch?"

I nod, and before I can say a word, he brushes his lips against my cheek and disappears into the crowd.

I turn back to my locker.

Homecoming.

Something I thought I'd never have.

And now it's mine.

I'm standing in Sienna's bedroom, surrounded by her pale pink walls. Sienna is in the attached bathroom, clanging around in the cabinets, searching for the perfect shade of lip gloss. As if she ever wears anything but cherry.

I can't stop staring at myself in the mirror, at the green silk dress I bought over two years ago on a whim. It's knee length, with a sweetheart neckline and an open back that makes me feel a little exposed.

Fifteen-year-old Lexi didn't mind being a little daring.

I remember buying this dress, the last weekend before school started for our sophomore year. Sienna talked me into it. Oh, sure, I loved it, would have jumped at the chance to wear it, but I only wanted to go to homecoming if Steven asked me. Sienna had no idea that's who I was waiting on, and how could I tell her?

And it was too soon to know if that fantasy would come true. That camping trip had been a week prior, and it seemed as if he liked me, but I was afraid I was reading too much into it.

God, I wanted it to be true. I wanted to discover that he did feel for me the way I felt for him. And I was afraid buying this dress—beautiful as it was—would jinx it somehow.

But I can't blame the dress for how all that worked out. I spin around, watch the fabric swirl around my knees, moving like the ocean.

Someone outside honks, and I take a few steps back to peer out the window. It's the limo, shiny black, shimmering under the spotlights mounted over the garage doors.

I walk to the door. "Sienna! Are you ready?"

She steps out of the bathroom, and it's hard not to stare. She's wearing a red satin dress with a short ruffled skirt that has black streaks running through it. The top has only one strap, the other shoulder bare. Her platinum hair is pulled up in a French twist that would look severe on anyone else. On her it looks elegant, understated in comparison to the outrageous dress. Topping it off is the simple diamond pendant dangling on a delicate silver chain.

The only jewelry I'm wearing is the blue and teal bracelet, which strangely, seems more green when matched with the dress, and a simple pear of pearl earrings my grandmother loaned me. She was so excited about me going to homecoming, I think she wanted to give me every piece of jewelry she owned.

"Do I look okay?"

I grin. "You look hot as hell, and you know it. Patrick won't know what hit him."

She smiles back at me. "You look perfect."

"Thanks." I look down at my dress, smoothing out wrinkles that aren't there. Tonight is about reclaiming what I lost, and I hope I can pull it off.

I slip on a pair of white strappy heels, unconcerned with their height. Erik is so much taller than me, it doesn't matter how many inches they are. Sienna and I make our way to the front door, our high heels clicking on the hardwood floors.

"We have to pick up Nikki on the way," Sienna says.

I nod, try not to wonder who she's going to homecoming with.

When we step into the cool October air, Erik and Patrick are climbing out of the limo. Erik looks like something on the posters outside the Tux Shop. His shoulders, chest, and arms perfectly fill out a jacket that would look loose and bulky on anyone else. Down to the shiny black shoes, he looks every inch the gentleman.

I find myself beaming as I walk up to him. He fits right into my fantasies. In his hands is a clear plastic box, and inside is a white iris surrounded by baby's breath. He's beaming, and any trace of butterflies disappears as I smile back.

It might be supernatural, this connection we have, but it's still real. He knows me in a way no one else ever has.

He pops the box open and retrieves the corsage. He secures it on my wrist, his fingers skimming along my skin. A different kind of butterflies spring forth. "You look stunning," he says.

"Thanks."

He leans down, tipping my chin back with his finger, and places a quick kiss on my lips. My jawline tingles where his fingers touched me. I'm smiling again. This can't be real. It's a fairy tale, something I thought I'd never have. But just like all the other fantasies—regular dates, visits to the lighthouse—it's real, something Erik has given me.

We climb into the limo, and I slide over to let Erik sit next to me. He puts a hand on my knee, and I can feel the heat of it through the satin skirt.

"Thanks for coming," I say.

"Wouldn't miss it for the world." He gives my knee a little squeeze.

Nikki's house isn't far from Sienna's; it's just down on River Walk Loop, a slightly less expensive version of Sienna's street.

I'm spacing out a little bit—marveling at the way my life has changed in just a month—when the limo pulls to a stop. I look out at the couple standing just beyond the expansive tinted windows—I can see them, but they can't see me—and what I see makes my blood run cold.

Nikki's date.

It's Cole. No. She can't do that to me.

He wouldn't do that to me.

But he did. He's standing right there with her.

Erik's grip on my knee tightens just a little. He's steady as a rock, next to me, as if he knows my insides are swirling painfully.

It's stifling in the limo as Cole swings the door open, and the two of them climb in, Cole's lanky frame bent over in the confines of the vehicle. He slides in next to Sienna, across from Erik and me. I avoid his eyes, but he keeps staring, as if he wants me to meet his look. As if he wants to see the hurt he's caused.

This is his revenge. I rubbed Erik in his face, and now he has Nikki to get me right back.

Nikki ignores me, putting her hand on Cole's thigh. "Thanks so much for my corsage. It's beautiful."

It's also a white iris, same as mine. My matching corsage burns on my wrist. There are only a few florists in town, but somehow I feel pathetic, wearing the same corsage as her. I want to yank it off my wrist and fling it across the limo.

Instead I sit quietly, my fingernails digging into my palm. Nikki seems to have finally picked up on the same unfortunate coincidence, because she's staring at her corsage, her eyes flickering over to me. I shift in the seat, glad that the high school is so close. I don't think I can handle being in this enclosed space for much longer. It's far too hot in here.

The second we arrive in the school lot, I nearly fall out of the car in a desperate attempt to get away from Cole and Nikki. Erik swoops in just in time to grab my arm and right me before I land on my knees.

"Are you okay?" he murmurs under his breath, close to my ear. His eyes dart back to Cole as if to tell me what he's *really* asking. I nod and let him maneuver his arm so he's escorting me instead of holding me up. It's a little cool for a short, flimsy gown like this, but it feels good after the claustrophobic heat of the limo.

We make our way across the concrete and through the glass double doors, our stiff formal shoes filling the air. Although I don't know for sure, I imagine Cole and Nikki boring holes into the back of my head with their eyes. They must have bonded over their equal hatred of me.

When we enter the already crowded school gym, I nod at Sienna even as I flee for safety within the crowd. My movements are erratic, but Erik never lets go of my arm.

He knows why I'm freaking out, and I feel terrible, putting him in this position. He knows he was the consolation prize, and I must be hurting him right now with my reaction. I try to get a hold of myself, but I just can't quite do it.

Even though *I* dumped *Cole,* somehow I never thought I'd have to see him with someone else. Sure, he was at the carnival, but I'd convinced myself they were there as friends. Somehow, I pictured him pining over me forever, as stupid as that sounds.

I wonder if he'll pick up his old girl-a-week habit because of me. If he'll go back to using girls the way he did before Steven died.

No, that's giving me too much credit, and him not enough.

When we reach the center of the throng, Erik spins me around, stopping me mid-yank. He pulls my arms up to rest on his shoulders as he tugs me close, his hands on my lower back. I let him get as close as he wants. I close my eyes and lean my face against Erik's wide chest. He smells like the ocean, fresh and a little briny. He must have left the windows open again in his house to smell so strongly like the sea.

I begin to unwind, as Erik and I sway to the music. Our motions are much slower than those of the couples around us. An electric, calming current seems to run between us.

"I know who he is to you," Erik finally murmurs.

"He's no one," I say, my voice barely audible above the music. It cracks. He knows the truth, so there's no use hiding it.

Erik softly squeezes. "I'm sorry it has to be like this."

"Me too."

We sway for a few moments in silence. "I fell in love once," he says.

I pull just far enough back to look up at Erik. His blue eyes have darkened like a storm, and he's looking at nothing in particular, lost in a memory.

"Her name was Kate. She was beautiful."

"What happened?"

Erik blinks and looks down at me, frowning. It doesn't look quite right on him—I've grown used to that smile of his. "Nothing."

"Nothing?"

He shakes his head, then pulls me closer again, until his chin rests on the top of my head. "How could it? I knew I'd only have to leave her, hurt her. I had to find *you*."

I swallow. "Oh."

"I'm almost certain she felt the same way for me, but I'll never know because I never let myself talk to her. It would have only taken one conversation, I'm sure of it, before I wouldn't have been able to leave her side."

"So you just watched her from afar? You don't think she was worth . . . trying?"

I feel him shake his head, give me a squeeze. "It gets easier, making the right choices. It just takes a little time. This will be worth it, I promise."

He pulls back enough that I can look up, see the sincere, adoring look in his eyes.

I thought I was over Cole. Everything with Erik has been going so well. I shouldn't be freaking out like this . . . Erik isn't such a bad consolation prize, is he? I could fall for him, if I'd just stop thinking of Cole long enough to do it.

He pulls me close as one song melts into the next. I rest my cheek against the lapel of his tuxedo. His arms tighten around my waist, and we turn a little bit, giving me a clear view of the one person I wanted to avoid: Cole.

I feel a painful stab to the chest as I watch him dance with Nikki. His back is to me, but I'd recognize his hair anywhere. They aren't dancing as closely as Erik and I are, but Nikki's arms are draped loosely over his shoulders. As they turn, I take in the way his hands rest on her hips. A weird, possessive fire takes root. I want to walk over and shove him off her.

Erik picks up on the change and leans down to murmur in my ear. "Do you want to go get our pictures taken?"

"Sure." I let his arms slide away from my waist, and we link hands, heading to the opposite side of the cafeteria. A short line has formed at the photo booth. It must be some kind of travel-the-world theme because one backdrop has Big Ben on it and another has the Eiffel tower.

We stand quietly, our fingers intertwined, waiting patiently for our turn. I look up at Erik and find myself smiling, despite it all.

Homecoming. Two years too late for Steven, but it finally arrived. It's so much like what they show in the movies . . . and yet so different, too. So vibrant and alive. I feel as if I'm watching it through goggles, through a viewfinder, as if I'll be able to rewind it and see it again and again.

Erik tugs my hand, and I follow him to the first available photo station, one with a giant Pyramid. We step up onto a white felt carpet. The photographer directs us so that Erik is standing behind me, his arms around my waist. My shoulders press back into his chest. I smile for the camera, a wide genuine smile, and the bright flash momentarily blinds me.

"Thank you. Your photographs will be ready on Monday at the main office." He hands me a slip with a number on it. I hand it to Erik, and he tucks it into the pocket of his slacks.

Erik pulls back the sleeve on his suit jacket. "I think we were going to dinner at eight," he says. "Should we find the others?"

"Sure. I'm starving," I say. "I didn't even catch where we were going, did you?"

"Barini's? Barelli's? Something like that."

I freeze.

His eyes narrow. "What? Is it no good?"

I shake my head, try to get rid of the pressure in my chest. "It's not the food. It's . . . it's on the waterfront."

I'm not tempted to pull Erik into the water, but I still swim and sing every night, and I don't know if I can handle sitting at a table with Cole and Patrick. And I don't want to find out.

His lips part, and he stands there for a second, as thrown off balance as I am. And then, "I'll take care of it."

"How?"

He leans in close, his gaze piercing mine. "Just give me ten minutes. Meet me at the door where we came in, okay?"

I nod, and then he gives my hand a squeeze before pushing his way through the crowd.

I'm standing in the entry to the cafeteria, arms crossed at my chest, when Sienna walks up. "Can you believe that?"

"Uh, no? What?" I glance at Erik, who trails behind her. He gives me a "just go along with it" sort of look.

"I made those reservations *three weeks* ago. How can they just give away our table like that?"

"Oh, uh, yeah. That sucks."

Sienna turns to look at Erik. "What made you think to call and check?"

He juts a thumb over his shoulder. "I heard a group of people talking about it when we were in line for pictures. Apparently, they overbooked the dining room. There was a big rehearsal dinner or something."

Sienna harrumphs. "I should call them, demand that they accommodate us."

Kristi shrugs. She has on a pretty, powder blue strapless dress. When she crosses her arms, it pushes her almost-there chest up. "I don't know . . . I told you I don't like seafood, but I was overruled. I think this is a sign you should have listened." She gives Sienna a pointed look. She loves that we can't go to Barelli's.

Nikki steps up, Cole beside her. Is his hand on her waist? I can't tell, without leaning over and being super obvious. "Where are we going to go then?"

Patrick nudges Sienna with his shoulder. "How about that fifties diner on Alder street?"

Sienna scoffs. "It's a *breakfast* diner. We'd have to eat pancakes." She pauses and motions to her attire. "And we're obscenely overdressed."

"I don't know. That sounds kind of funny," Erik says. "Way more memorable than a fancy restaurant. *Everyone* goes somewhere fancy for homecoming."

Kristi grins. "Pancakes sound awesome right about now."

Sienna raises a brow and gives us all a skeptical look. As annoyed as she is over the circumstances, I can tell she loves that she's in charge. "Seriously? I guess it does sound kind of fun. Everyone will stare, of course, because who eats pancakes in tuxedoes?" She purses her lips. The idea is growing on her. "What do you think?"

She's looking at me. I grin, relief flooding through me. "I'm in."

"Okay, the diner on Alder it is," she says. "I can't believe we're having pancakes for homecoming dinner."

She turns around and leads the way out of the dance, a queen with her head held high. Erik joins me at the back of the group. The sound of the music disappears behind us as we leave the dance.

"*Thank you*," I mouth.

"*You're welcome*," he whispers, squeezing my hand.

We end up at an enormous U-shaped table, the biggest booth at the diner. Sienna was right, of course; the other patrons keep shooting us looks, trying to figure out what a bunch of kids in tuxedoes and ball gowns are doing at a diner where the priciest meal costs $8.99.

Not surprisingly, Sienna's getting a total kick out of all the attention. And I'm so relieved to be this far from the shore that I can't stop smiling either. I have to stop myself from saying thank you to Erik about a thousand times.

I don't know what I would have done if my date had been anyone else. How I would have avoided eating dinner right on top of the ocean. Just thinking about it nearly sends me into full-on panic. But then I force myself back to the reality of Erik and the black-and-white-checkered table in front of us, and all I feel is relief.

Patrick pulls a Trivial Pursuit question out of the giant box on the table. "In what month does the Kentucky Derby take place?"

"May!" Sienna shouts.

Kristi gives her a look.

"What? My parents go every year. My turn!" She picks up a card, then scowls. "Well this is lame," she says. "What decade saw names first begin to appear on the back of NFL—"

"The fifties," Erik answers without pause. "It was the 1950s."

I think Cole just rolled his eyes, but I can't tell from here.

"Impressive," she says, shoving the card into the end of the box.

Before Erik can respond, the waitress walks up and gives us a stack of menus. As the others choose their drinks, I turn to Erik. "You like sports?"

He shrugs. "What guy doesn't?"

"Huh. I didn't realize you were *so* into football."

He leans in, lowers his voice. "There's a lot you don't know about me." He whispers in my ear. "But you have plenty of time to learn."

He's right. We have all the time in the world. Yet for some reason, the idea makes me feel a little restless. "I'm going to go to the restroom. I'll be right back."

I slide out of the booth and walk around the big L-shaped counter, ducking into the bathroom at the back of the restaurant. I don't actually have to use the restroom, so I just wash my hands, staring at my decked-out reflection in the mirror. I marvel at how pretty the dress is. I spin around, admiring it. When I come to a stop, though, it feels a little melancholy.

I was supposed to wear this for Steven.

I dry my hands, tossing the paper towel into the trashcan as I exit the bathroom.

I nearly walk right into Cole.

"Oh!" I start, then back up. I go to move past him, but he touches my arm, and I go still.

"It's not real."

"What?"

"Your smile. When you look at him. It's nothing like the one you had for Steven."

I look up at him, the breath gone from my lungs. "You're just saying that because it's not you."

He shakes his head. "Don't do that. Don't pretend like I'm the only one who felt something."

I cross my arms. "I'm with Erik, and you're with Nikki."

"I'm *friends* with Nikki."

I hate the surge of relief I feel at his words. "It doesn't matter."

Cole leans in closer. "Why? *Why* doesn't it matter? It's the only thing that *does* matter."

I scowl. "I don't want to talk about it."

"And that pretty well sums up the problem, doesn't it?"

Anger sparks inside me. "Why do you keep doing this?"

"Because I've wanted to be with you for three years, okay? That's why."

I feel as if he's punched me in the stomach. "But that's—"

"The day I met you. At Sienna's house. Steven and I were playing Ping-Pong and you and Sienna walked in off the beach. You were twisting your wet hair up into a ponytail, and then you saw us, and you smiled. . . ."

"Then why didn't you—"

"Because you were smiling for *him*. And I would have had to have been an idiot to get in between that. And that's why I know whatever you feel for Erik, it's nothing like what you had for Steven. And nothing like what I feel for you."

I look away, blinking rapidly. "If you liked me for so long, why did you wait until now?"

Cole gives me a bitter smile. "Because even when he was dead, I couldn't compete with Steven."

I step away from him. "I need to go back to the table." I don't wait for him to respond.

After we're all stuffed full of eggs, bacon, and pancakes, we pile back into the limo to go home. Erik's house is the first stop, barely ten minutes away. The limo doesn't fit in the small driveway, so it stops half in the street.

Before Erik climbs out, he turns to me. "Come over in the morning? For breakfast, part two?"

I nod, blushing as he leans in and kisses me in front of everyone. I can't help but feel Cole's eyes on me, watching as Erik steps out of the limo. I don't have to look at him to know what his expression is.

The limo stays silent for the ride to my house, which thankfully only takes moments. I all but spring out, mumbling, "Thank you" and "I had a great time." As quickly as I can, I slam the door so I won't see Cole's face behind the dark tint of the glass.

They all think I'm going to bed. Instead, I creep into the house, standing outside of my Gram's door for a long moment, listening to the heavy snoring through her door.

Then I change my clothes, and minutes later I'm starting my car. It's time to swim.

CHAPTER TWENTY-SEVEN

The next morning, I leave a note for Gram and dash off to Erik's house, my hair still wet with lake water.

When he answers the door, I swear smoke pours out. "Uh, I'm not much of a cook," he says, with an adorable sheepish grin. "I make no claims that the food you are about to eat is edible in any way."

I laugh. He's wearing gray track pants and a long-sleeved T-shirt, his hair sticking up slightly in the back.

I smile and inhale the aroma. The smell sweeps in memories of my mother, a terrible cook, whose only mastery in the kitchen was chicken-noodle. "I'll cut you a little slack."

He smiles. "How very generous of you. The first batch of pancakes isn't bad, actually. And the bacon is only two levels past crispy."

He pulls a covered plate from the microwave and reveals a stack of slightly misshapen flapjacks. "I bought the breakfast stuff before I knew we were also having breakfast for dinner. So, uh, sorry for the, uh, redundancy there."

"No worries. I could eat my weight in pancakes and still want more."

He smiles. "I thought we could eat on the porch. I brought some juice and utensils out already. Grab some pancakes."

I take a clean plate off the stack and serve up the top three pancakes. He leads me out to the back porch, picking up a small fleece blanket along the way. As soon as the door opens, the whooshing sound of the ocean greets my ears. I sit down beside him, pulling the throw blanket over my lap.

From behind the house, the sun basks the beach in a warm glow. But we're all alone, despite the intense beauty of the vista. The sand is empty of any people or birds. It's like this little beach house is on an island, not the edge of town.

I lean slightly on him, and take my first bite of pancakes. "They taste better than they look," I say, between bites.

"Thanks. I think."

Ten quiet minutes later, he takes my empty plate and stacks it up on his. Then he sets it on the small table beside the rocker. I pull my feet up underneath me. He keeps his on the ground, rocking us as he wraps an arm around me. I sigh, staring out at the beach as I lean back against the porch swing and wrap the blanket tighter around the two of us.

The morning seems extraordinarily quiet. Beyond the rustling of the reed grass and the breath of the ocean, there's nothing.

"Did you have fun last night?" I ask, leaning my head against his chest.

"I did," he says. "I could spend every night seeing you in a dress that short."

I laugh. "It's nice, though, doing . . . normal stuff."

"Yeah, definitely," he says.

We go quiet again, and I stare out at the ocean. Moments tick past. Waves come in and out. Birds swoop down and fly away.

And I can't think of anything to say. It's weird, how if we're not talking about our curses, we don't really have that much to say. I guess I never noticed that before.

Far in the distance, white clouds appear, but for now, most of the sky is blue.

"Beautiful," he finally says.

"Definitely," I agree.

"I meant you."

I look down at my hands, feeling silly. "Oh."

He pulls me even closer, rests his lips against the spot where the curve of my neck meets my shoulder. "I love you," he says.

The ocean goes as silent as my heart. I swallow. It's everything I've always desperately wanted to hear. Someone *loves me*.

But I feel strangely trapped by the words. Like the best thing I could do right now is leave.

These last few weeks, that was what this was all about. That was why we were spending time together—so we could fall in love. His birthday is days away, now. So why does it surprise me so much to hear it? How did I manage to forget that being with Erik wasn't just about having a normal teen experience . . . but about falling in love with him?

I can feel his breath on my skin. "This is the part where you say—"

"Why?"

He lifts his head, tries to look me in the eyes, but I don't turn away from the beach. "That wasn't where I was going with that."

I sigh but still don't meet his eyes. "I know. But why do you love me?"

"What do you mean? I love everything. You're amazing."

It's hard not to frown. "No, I mean, what do you love *best* about me?"

God, how pathetic do I sound? It's like I'm fishing for compliments. But for some reason it seems inordinately important. I have to know why he loves me.

He goes so silent. I wouldn't even think he was beside me if his arms weren't wrapped around me. "You're beautiful. And smart."

A small lump grows in my throat. I'm *cursed* to be beautiful. He should know that's the wrong thing to say. And smart? It rings false. Erik and I have never had one intellectual conversation. He's never even asked me what my other classes are besides English. He doesn't know they're AP courses. So why would he think I'm smart?

Something twists in my chest.

Either he only loves me because I can give him a normal life—because I'm his match—or he doesn't really love me at all; he's just saying it.

I wonder, if Cole could have loved me, what he would have said if I asked the same question. It wouldn't have been "because you're smart," I know that much.

I smile and look up at him, hoping he buys it.

CHAPTER TWENTY-EIGHT

After nearly twenty minutes in relative silence—in which we both simply swing back and forth, staring out at the ocean—things become uncomfortable. Those three little words are jammed between us. I wonder if he's still waiting for me to say them back.

I consider telling Erik not to worry about it, that we can pretend he didn't say it, but I don't know if that would make things better or worse.

Finally, when I can't take it any longer, Erik speaks. "Sienna mentioned Port Street last night."

"Oh?"

He nods. "I was thinking we could wander around there today. It sounds fun."

I nod. I'm relieved, because he's acting like nothing happened, as if he didn't just say something that requires an answer I didn't give.

Port Street is the boardwalk area, super close to where the festival was. It's the tourist trap, filled with its saltwater taffy stands, antique shops, and souvenir stores stuffed with things like dried-up sea stars, vials of dyed beach sand, wooden sailboats, and kites.

And that's why twenty minutes later, I'm standing there, finding it a little ironic that he'd bring me to the most ocean-centric place in this whole town, but I try to think of it in a different way.

He's trying to do *normal* things. Things our classmates have done all their lives. Hang out. See the sights. Besides that, he knows how obsessed I am with the ocean. I hate it because of my curse, but he thinks just because there's hope that he can cure the curse, I'm free to love it.

It rubs me the wrong way that he's never asked if that's how it is for me. He assumes I love it, but he seems to have forgotten it's still the place where I killed someone.

Why hasn't he ever asked what happened that night? Why has he never asked who I was before he came here?

But I've never asked him, either. I never thought of who he was at his old school.

Was I so dazzled by living a normal life that I never looked at the guy standing right next to me?

Erik pulls me along the sidewalk, and I try to stop thinking about . . . about everything. He's trying. He really is. And he loves me. Or so he thinks.

But I still don't know how I feel about him. The past few weeks have been like a fairy tale, but there's a reason fairy tales aren't real. They seem . . . amazing in the books. But who bothers looking beyond the surface? Who even knows anything about Cinderella's

Prince Charming—other than he's a handsome prince?

This morning's confession has suddenly shoved that all in my face.

I swallow and try to turn my attention to the place Erik is pulling me toward. I've lived in this town so long, and yet it's been years since I've walked this particular strip. The left side of the street has the shops and restaurants. The right side is the marina, where the chartered fishing boats are always moored. At this time of the year, things are quieter, most of the boats sitting idly along the docks, the salt water lapping at the sides of the boats.

My hand rests in Erik's, our fingers intertwined. It feels different today. Like he's holding on tighter.

I wore a long sundress today, one with quarter-length sleeves and a skirt that graces my ankles. It's a little cool for it, so I added a cardigan, and some cute flats. I guess I'm wishing for summer, something more carefree. Erik is wearing Doc Martens, dark indigo jeans, and a deep hunter green sweater. The sweater's short zipper is left undone, so that the wide collar falls over his shoulders. We must make a cute couple, the two of us. Him, with his Adonis good looks, and me, the siren, always pretty no matter what. Every time he turns toward me, smiling in that warm, happy way of his, I have to catch my breath—his eyes remind me so much of my own.

He's been so sweet, trying to fit into my clique, taking me on so many dates. He's done everything I've asked for, and he's never asked for anything of his own. So why don't I feel more strongly about him?

Erik and I walk into a gift shop. He lets go of my hand and walks over to the saltwater taffy. He raises one of his dark, thick eyebrows at me and nods in the direction of the taffy. I shrug and then nod, so he grabs one of the clear bags and a big metal scoop, and sets to work dumping a mixture of flavors into the bag.

I wouldn't have pegged him as a taffy kind of guy. For some reason that fact sticks in my head. I don't know what kind of candy he likes. Whether he's from a big family. What the last eighteen years have been like in his life, if they've been filled with as much tragedy and heartache as my own. He said his dad is a nix and his mom is a siren. . . . Are they still in love? Does *he* love *them*?

I turn away and walk across the room, picking up the various overpriced novelties. I start with a sand dollar. It's smooth, flawless. I run my thumb over the top of it, staring at the star in the center. It was alive once.

I plunk it back down in the bin. This whole section is stocked with sea stars, shells, even dried-up puffer fish and sea horses. It's ugly in its beauty. I want to throw the whole bin in the trash even as I want to buy everything, bring them to the beach, and find some way to make them alive again.

If sirens were smaller, more plentiful, maybe they'd dry me up and put me in a bin right next to the seashells.

Erik walks up, wraps an arm around me as if it's the most natural thing in the world and holds up the bag of taffy. I nod. He doesn't even glance at the bins next to me.

I watch him walk away and remember what he looked like in the tuxedo last night. And then I think about how I've spent the last hour with Erik, acting like a normal teen, the one thing I've always wanted.

And yet despite all of Erik's promises, everything he's given me, I feel strangely . . . unfulfilled. Restless. Sometimes, being with Erik is no different than being the ice queen. He doesn't push me like Cole does. Doesn't want to know what I'm afraid of.

He doesn't even know who I am, and yet it doesn't seem to bother him. It's not about who I am to him.

It's about *what* I am.

Erik takes his bag of taffy and leads me outside. My flats slap against the pavement as he pulls me up against his hip. Again, he smiles in that warm, inviting way of his that always seems to put me at ease. His smile is like wading into the water for the first time in hours.

I smile back at him as he opens the door to an ice-cream parlor for me, and I step into the artificially bright space. He's talking. His lips are moving as he stares straight at me.

And then I realize I haven't heard a word of what he's said to me in the last ten minutes.

And then I realize he hasn't noticed.

CHAPTER TWENTY-NINE

Erik and I walk back to his place, taking the beach route as we stroll hand in hand. I feel weird about it, and want to pull my hand from his, but he seems to have forgotten about our awkward moment this morning and I don't want him to think of it now.

My shoes dangle from my fingertips. My bare toes sink into the sand, the grains sticking in between them. The sand suddenly seems deeper, thicker, like it's trying to suck me right into the beach.

Erik is the only way I can have everything I've ever wanted. The only way to guarantee I never turn into my mom. Without him, I'll never be able to keep Cole and all the others safe.

It's only with Erik I can be normal. But I wish he cared more about who I was. Wish he asked me about things that mattered. Favorite ice cream? That's easy. What about my biggest fear? Greatest hope? Doesn't he care about those things?

This only works if I can love him . . . and what if I can't?

Because with Erik, it's so easy to keep him at arm's length. So easy to keep everything skin deep, never looking beyond that.

Never falling. With him, everything is about the curse, and nothing is about . . .

Me.

We get back to the beach house and thunk down on the couch, and I feel more tired than ever. Erik rubs my shoulders as we sit in the quiet, the sounds of the ocean rushing in through the open windows. I've never felt so totally worn down, exhausted. I want to curl up in a ball and let the world pass me by.

"You okay?" He leans forward, traces his lips along my neck, his breath hot on my skin. *You okay?* just reminds me of Cole. Of all his questions. Of the way he met my eyes and seemed to look deep into my soul, wanting a real answer. Why do I feel like Erik is asking that just because he thinks he should? Why do I feel as though he doesn't want an answer at all?

I have no reason to think that. He's never done anything wrong. Not specifically anyway.

I nod, but I don't speak.

"You've seemed a little . . . off since this morning," he says. He doesn't add "since I said I love you," but I know he's thinking it. I look down at my hands, wring them together. My mouth is so dry it's like someone jammed an entire package of cotton balls down my throat.

"Erik . . ." My voice trails off, weak and quiet.

"Yeah?" He gives me a squeeze, then leans back again, relaxes against the couch.

I relish that I finally have a little room to breathe. "Do you ever feel like . . . like maybe there should be something more?"

The air turns heavy, the silence deafening. I imagine him staring at the back of my head, blinking over and over.

"More than what?"

I twist the blue bracelet in circles around my wrist. "I don't know. Like . . . like this should be . . . deeper or something." I twist around to look him in the eye. "Like . . . chemistry. Some deeper pull, or desire, or . . . something."

Jeez, I'm butchering this.

I shift around, trying to get comfortable, but there's no position that makes this any easier. And it doesn't matter anyway. Wherever I go, I can feel his eyes boring into my skin.

"Is this about seeing Cole with Nikki at the dance?"

"What? No. I mean . . . not really. I don't know." I slide away from him and sit on the other side of the couch. I need to see him, to face him directly so that I don't have to guess as at his expression. "Doesn't it kind of feel like we're trying too hard here? Would you even care about me at all if I weren't a siren?"

His lips part, his eyes flaring a bit. "What? Of course I would. I told you . . . I love you. It's not about you being a siren." He sits back and looks away for a second, out at the beach through the big picture window. Then he looks back at me just as quickly. "Is that what you're worried about? That I don't care about you? Or that I only do because of what you are?"

"Well . . . yeah. I just don't know if this is real, you know? Or if we're just forcing it."

Erik slides over on the couch, making up the distance between us. He takes my hands in his. "I promise you, this is all very real to me. You're . . . *amazing*. Sweet and beautiful and smart. It's not about being a siren, I swear. I mean, sure, that's what brought me to you. But I never would have stayed if I didn't think this could be something real."

I let out a long breath of air through my lips, then look up at him, into the dark blue eyes that remind me so much of what's in the mirror. "I just feel like I need to know you. As a person not as . . . a nix."

He nods. "Of course."

"Do you think . . . do you think maybe we could slow this all down?"

His eyebrows furrow. "What do you mean?"

"I mean, this all happened so fast, and I can't keep up because we are together so much and everything is constantly changing. I just need time to process it. I just want a few nights to go back to my swimming and hanging with my Grandma and let everything just . . . settle in, you know? I just feel really out of sorts, and I need time to adjust." My voice has a hint of a quiver in it. I don't even know why I'm doing this, what I want. Guilt pools in my stomach when I see his stricken expression.

He reaches out and grasps my hand. "Are you sure? My eighteenth is coming up, and how will you fall for me in time if we're not together? I can't kill someone, Lexi. I *can't*."

He's squeezing my hand too hard. I pull it away, and then I stand. "Please. Just a couple days, okay? Let me adjust to this. I'm not leaving you, I swear."

He stands, but I put out a hand, and he reluctantly sits back down. "Two days?"

I nod, the lump growing in my throat.

"Okay," he says. "I can handle two days. But my birthday is barely a week away. I can't give you much longer."

"Thank you," I say. I lean forward, brush my lips against his. He grabs my cheek with one hand, his fingers curving behind my head, and pulls me closer, until our kiss lingers so long I'm out of breath.

I pull away from him, the taste of him lingering on my lips. "I'll be back in a couple of days," I say.

"Until then," he says. I nod, and then leave him sitting there on the couch, surrounded by the ocean's scent.

CHAPTER THIRTY

That night, I park my car in the usual spot, noticing the Jeep parked next to a tree.

It's Erik's. He's sitting in the driver's seat of his darkened car, watching me. Shadows hang over his eyes, making them impossible to see.

He matches my stare, and I sit, teeth gritted, hands gripping the wheel so hard it's painful. Long moments tick past as we look at each other, neither of us moving. What is he doing here? He was supposed to give me space. I know he was scared, but it's just two days. I wasn't leaving him. I just wanted a little time to think.

I watch him through the shadows as he unbuckles his seat belt. I don't get out of the car as he slides out of his bucket seat and walks to my door. I unroll the window.

"Hi," he says, looking sheepish.

"Why are you here?" My voice comes out a little angry. I lower it. "I thought you were going to give me a couple of days."

He looks down at the key ring dangling from a finger. "I know, but I just got a little worried you were pulling away."

"Erik. Seriously. I need some space."

"Are you sure?"

"Yes." It's hard not to shout it.

"Okay, I'm sorry, I didn't mean to come up here, but before I knew it I was driving up the gravel road."

I set a hand on his. "Please. Just give me a couple of days. I swear it will all work out. Okay?"

"Sure." He leans in and gives me a long, lingering kiss, and I feel my body react to it. As he walks away, I can't help but wonder if that's what he intended. If maybe he thought the kiss would make me change my mind, want him to stay with me. I sit in my car and watch him back up. I don't move until his headlights have disappeared down the gravel road.

In fact, I don't move for a long time, my eyes fixated on the spot where I last saw his red taillights glow.

Erik is taking this all really hard. I get it, I do, but I don't like it.

I finally unsnap my seat belt and get out of the car. It's colder than I realized. I reach back into my Toyota and grab a black quilted jacket with a fur-lined hood. Then I put it on and zip it up to my chin. I shove my hands in the pockets and walk to the tree line, entering the shadowed darkness under the canopy. My sneakers sink in the thick pine-needle walkway, and the ferns I brush up against dampen my jeans. I take in several deep breaths through my nose, relishing the sweet smell of the damp forest.

I walk slowly today, in no hurry to get to the lake. The urge to sing is building, bubbling up to the surface as I make the trek through the woods.

The hunger for the water is just as strong as it's ever been.

The darkness seems thicker than usual somehow. Like the misting rain and the velvet sky have melded together into a big blanket. By the time I step into the clearing beside the lake, the urge to sing has grown enough that I shiver in anticipation.

I shed my clothing and step into the familiar waters, quickly diving under the surface. I stay underwater even longer than normal, until my lungs scream for oxygen. The icy water wraps around my skin, but I don't feel cold. I feel as though I'm sitting in a warm bath, every muscle relaxing in the water.

I finally come up for air, and my face barely breaks the surface when the song bursts free, my voice loud and clear as I let loose with a melody more haunting than the one that I've sung every night these last few weeks.

I'm only a half lap in when the song dies, and something doesn't feel right.

I jerk upright, glance across the lake at my tree. My clothes still dangle there, but Erik's not standing next to them. I blink, then spin around and scan the shore and the tree line.

No Erik.

And then something clicks into place. It feels like when I killed Steven. Like the desire to sing hasn't just disappeared, but like some deep need has been met. It's the same strange high that drove me to laugh and splash, feeling weirdly euphoric, while Steven floated facedown, just a few dozen yards from me.

Sudden, rushing panic courses through me. The silence buzzes in my ears as my stomach begins to flip over and over and over.

I twist around, then around again, desperate to figure out where *he* is. Whoever he is.

And that's when I see the body.

"No!" I scream, the sound more like a wildcat's scream than my voice. I throw everything into swimming toward the body floating hardly twenty feet from me, facedown, innocent as driftwood. I don't even stop to see who it is. I just flip the body over and yank on the collar of the shirt, dragging him behind me as I kick, gaining momentum until the water streams by faster than ever. My feet find the ground, and I struggle to get him up onto the shore. For the first time, I look down at the pale face and am met with my worst nightmare.

Cole.

Nooo. An animal scream wrenches from my throat. Not Cole. Anyone but Cole.

Oh God, no. How did it come to this? I did everything in my power to keep him away from the lake, away from me. I can't have killed him. I can't go through the pain of killing someone again.

Cole's once beautiful hazel eyes are glassy and lifeless, staring upward. His dark curls are plastered to his forehead and temples. His skin is ashy, clammy. He's not breathing.

I pound on his chest without even thinking. Pinching his nose, I force air into his lungs. It's exactly like those desperate moments with Steven, when I tried to bring him back, before I realized that the life had left his once strong body.

This can't happen. Not again. I won't let it. I can't do this, not to Cole, not to the only person who's tried to get to know me, the real me, in the last two years.

Though I'm breathless myself, I don't stop. I push against his chest several more times. Just as I lean over to force more air into his lungs, water slides between his lips. And suddenly, he's coughing.

I jump up and step back, watching as he rolls onto his side, hacking hard, coughing up water. He's curled over in a fetal position, gasping for breath.

Before I understand what I'm doing, I'm backing up, sliding my clothes off the branch behind me and retreating into the shadows. He pulls his knees underneath him and kneels, still coughing, one hand gripping his stomach, the other sinking into the rocky, muddy shore.

Once the coughing slows, and I know he's going to be okay, I slip further into the shadows. I disappear, my bare feet picking up a sprint. I dodge tree limbs and roots and rocks, bursting into a frantic run, wishing I could leave the truth behind as easily as I leave Cole hacking up lake water.

The gravel bites into my bare feet, punishing me for my mistakes.

I almost killed.

Sickening dread swirls in my stomach, nearly making me vomit as I reach my car.

I almost killed.

I yank the door open and fall into the seat. Then I curl up into a ball and close my eyes, rocking back and forth.

I almost killed.

CHAPTER THIRTY-ONE

I stay home sick from school the next day. And in a way, it's true: I am sick. Sick of the curse. Sick of my life.

I can't face Cole right now. Not when I know what nearly happened. What I nearly did.

I stay in bed all day as my grandmother's television blares in the living room. The bowl of soup she gave me sits, cold, on the nightstand next to my bed.

I grip the toy Chevelle in my hand, my thumb sliding over the wheels. Cole nearly joined Steven, six feet under. Because I was too afraid to tell him what I was.

I am supposed to be empty of all feelings, empty of all life. That's what sirens are in the myths. Killing machines, bent on revenge. But if that's true, why does the pain in my chest overwhelm me? And why is it that what I want most can't be met by the siren's call?

Even Erik wasn't enough. He was drawn to me just because I was a siren. And that makes him like all the others, even if he knew what he was doing. He wanted me to fix him, and he wanted the life I could give him, but he never really wanted me.

But Cole is different.

And that's why I'm afraid to see him right now. As long as I don't face him, as long as I don't do what I have to do, I can still have the possibility of him. The daydream that he doesn't sneer and walk away.

But now I know I can't keep living like this.

I have to tell him.

Tears brim, and I let them slide down my temple, unbidden.

Nothing. That's what the women in my family get in the end. The guys always leave us far behind when they find out the truth. I don't know that I can survive that.

I let the tears swallow me whole as I mourn everything I know I'm going to lose once Cole knows.

But then it hits me: Maybe he already does. Maybe he saw me before he drowned, before he mindlessly walked into the lake.

The dreams and hopes that had swelled and grown in the last few weeks shrivel up and die, drowning in my tears.

I turn on my side and hug a pillow against me and let the sobs rack my body, crying so hard it becomes difficult to breathe. I squeeze my eyes shut and wish I could rewind the last month, find the strength to tell him what I should have to begin with.

The next morning, I stand outside the school's main doors. I didn't swim last night, which is enough to put me in a foul mood. I nearly went to my lake, but I wasn't sure what I'd do if Erik were there. If I'd let him hug me, try to take away the pain.

I'm weak. Too weak. And so I stayed away. And now I have a day of classes to get through, and it's only eight o'clock. I don't know how I'm going to manage. All I know is that tonight, after all of this is over, I have to go see Cole.

I take in a slow breath and push the heavy entry door open, step into the bustling hallway. Students stream past me, jostling to get to class. They don't even notice the change in my eyes as they pass me, don't see that I'm struggling to stay on my feet. I grit my teeth against the pain. It feels as if the carpeted halls are really a gauntlet of broken glass and sharp tin cans splitting the soles of my feet open.

Out of nowhere, a hand clamps onto my wrist. Cold, hard, unwelcome.

I spin around, steeling myself.

But it's not Cole. It's Erik. He gives me the strangest look. His eyes are sort of glossed over, a flash of resentment in them. "You were supposed to come over this morning."

I reach over with my free hand and wrench loose his grip on my arm. "I know, I'm sorry. I've had some things to deal with." I take in his strangely haughty look. I almost don't recognize him right now. "Look, I'll talk to you about this later. Soon, okay? Just not right now. I have too much going on."

That same look flares again, and something inside me shrinks back. I feel a little guilty, but I need to just get through today, make sure Cole is alive and breathing.

I'm still standing close to Erik, so close it wouldn't take a single step for me to kiss him, when Cole's hazel eyes come into focus. The second they meet mine, he tears his gaze away and stalks down the hall. Everything inside me hollows out.

A shrill bell rings, and my headache becomes splitting.

That evening, as the sun leaves orange streaks across the skyline, I stand on the beach outside Cole's house, my bones and limbs still aching. I watch the shadows in his room move behind the curtains. Thirty minutes more, and I'll have to go. The glow of the sunset seems extreme, illuminating the massive storm clouds building behind me.

The moon should be popping up by now, but the giant bank of clouds blocks it out. I need to swim soon, but I can't bring myself to leave.

An autumn storm rolls in, and lightning strikes over the ocean, illuminating the sky. Wind whips through my hair, and it streams out behind me, wild and unruly, a moving mass of waves. The cold bites through my blue sweater, but still I stand, and still I stare.

The door to Cole's room swings open. I consider moving, hiding, but I don't. I watch him step onto the small deck attached to his room, staying close to the house where the overhang will protect him from the sudden onslaught of raindrops that fall all around me.

One . . . Two . . .

Lightning streaks across the blackened sky, and for one bright moment, I know Cole can see me.

He reaches back and flips the porch light off, engulfing him in shadows as he steps forward into the downpour. His gray T-shirt darkens instantly.

My sweater is soaked through as well, and even my sneakers are wet enough that I can feel the rain on my toes. It's the sort of rain that soaks you through in seconds, turns your hair to dripping, tangled ropes. I should move. Run. Hide. But I stay rooted as he steps off the deck and into the dunes, as the wind continues to howl.

He climbs over the small sandy hills and crosses the short expanse of reed grass. Before I can react, he's standing right there in front of me, rain dripping from his hair. His T-shirt clings to the muscles on his shoulders and chest.

"What the hell are you doing?" He has to shout to be heard.

But he's talking to me. Hope soars in my chest, only to fall at the look in his eyes.

I shouldn't be here, shouldn't want this. I nearly killed him, and yet here I am anyway, as if once I tell him what I am—once he realizes it was me at the lake—he's going to give me another chance. It's impossible, but still I have to know.

I just can't stop myself from wanting to be with him. Maybe it's fate, that he found my lake, went back again. I don't know why he was there, but all that's important is that he was.

He's the only thing that's ever mattered. He's the only person I've wanted to be close to ever since I knew the truth about myself.

It's him or no one.

Lightning streaks again, but neither of us flinch. The lightning and thunder seem to be right on top of each other now, and yet we don't move, don't break our piercing stares.

"Just answer me one thing!" he yells. The storm nearly swallows his words, ripping them away on the gust of wind. He steps closer and a bead of rainwater slides down the bridge of his nose, drips off. He's standing so close it lands on the toe of my shoe.

"Did you ever really care about me? At all?"

My lip betrays me by trembling. I resist the urge to step back, retreat. Instead I nod as tears mix with the rain sliding down my cheeks. It's hard to breathe. I just sniffle.

The anger in his eyes melts, and he reaches out, as if to wipe away the tears. But at the last second, he seems to realize it's futile. He cups my cheek instead.

"Then why, Lexi? Why are you with him?"

I open my mouth to say something, anything to keep him here with me, but a booming thunderclap rumbles, followed almost instantly by lightning.

I make a decision right then and there. One that will finally tell me if this will ever truly work. I grab him by the T-shirt and pull him closer, shouting into his ear, "I can't explain. But I can show you. Grab your iPod."

We sit in my car near the lake, shivering. He from the cold, and me . . . from fear.

My mother played this game once. And it didn't go well. She showed my dad who she was, and he only ran. It hurts now when I think of it. I never connected with her, never understood her, couldn't see why she made the choices she did.

But I get it now. Because the same blind hope surges through me. My head and my heart don't agree. And I'm following my heart. I'm playing with fire, and I know if this all blows up, it's going to be as bad for me as it was for her. But I can't have Cole unless I tell him my secrets.

Lying nearly got him killed. It got my mother's boyfriend killed. Lying is a dangerous game.

Maybe I won't be able to have him even when he knows the truth about me either. But I have to try. I can't live like this anymore, not without giving it a shot.

He's the only thing that makes me feel alive.

"Are you ready?" I say, nearly in a whisper. The rain has quieted, leaves only tiny streaks on the windows. Cole is wearing a jacket now, but I haven't bothered to change out of my damp sweater and jeans. My toes are wet inside my sneakers, chafing around the edges.

He peers at me in the darkness. "I don't understand why we're here."

"You will. Come on." I push my door open, and it lets out its usual squeak, only now it sounds like a death knell. It's not too late to change my mind, pretend I brought him here just to see a lake that looks like a dozen others around here. But that won't solve anything. That won't give me Cole.

The rain is little more than a light mist now, and the patchy clouds allow us to see where we're going by the light of the moon. Funny, how quickly storms pass this close to the ocean.

Cole trips on a root and knocks into me. He's not used to these paths, can't navigate his way in the darkness as well as I can. He must have brought a flashlight last night. When he trips again, I take his hand, savor the feeling of it in mine as I lead him by memory. The canopy of the forest blots out the remaining light.

"Wait," he says, pulling me to a stop. "I've been here before—"

"I know," I say, yanking him back to a walk. I have to get this over with before I change my mind.

His hand is warm in mine, and it's almost too much. I want to turn around and pin him to a tree and kiss him with everything I have. But instead, I force myself to keep walking, to ignore the humming of my veins.

We emerge into the clearing, and the lake shines under the light of the moon.

"I was just here. Two nights ago . . ." Cole says, a little in awe. "It was so strange, I—"

"I know," I say. "That's what this is about. I saw you at this lake over a month ago. Why did you come?"

"I come up here a lot. Not this lake, specifically, but the forest. Just to get away from things. I got turned around that night, ended up here when I should have been on my way home, but it was peaceful and I didn't want to leave. If you were here, then why didn't you—"

"Because I didn't want you to come back. But you did. You don't understand—this is my lake."

He furrows his brow. "But it's part of the park system. At least, I thought it was. One of my favorite trails is just a little further down the gravel road. But this lake is not on the maps."

"I know. That's why it's mine."

Cole looks like he's going to say something, then stops himself, looking out at the lake again. I pull him over to the tree where I stood that night I watched him. I can feel it all as if it just happened:

the bark digging into my nails, the fury boiling in my veins.

Maybe if I'd known who he'd become to me, how much I'd come to love him, I could have avoided all of this. Instead, I am about to do the one thing I thought I would never do.

Risk everything for a boy.

I guess it's just the way we are, us sirens. Craving love above all else. Unable to function once we find it. But I refuse to think that everything I have with Cole is as simple as that. He's one of a kind. I need him. Want him.

Love him.

"Do you want to know what really happened with Steven?"

He searches my eyes, and I just stare right back at him, no longer trying to hide all my secrets. Then he nods.

I look down at the mud between our feet for a long second, taking in a deep breath. I have to do this. I *have* to. I nearly killed him by hiding the truth.

The words I'd been trying so long to keep inside rush out in one quick burst. "At around eleven that night, at the party, Steven invited me upstairs. I followed him out to the deck, but when I stepped out there, I could hardly hear his voice, because it was like the ocean was raging in my ears. I had this . . . inexplicable need to go swimming. So I asked him to go with me, down to the beach."

The expression on his face seems frozen, like it's taking everything he has just to listen to me. The darkness all around us has created odd shadows, and I'm not sure I can see his expression quite right.

I swallow. The story is only going to get worse. "We went down to the beach, and I felt this weird, excited giddiness. It was like an adrenalin rush, but a thousand times stronger. We stripped down and got in the water. Except as soon as I was in, I swam away from him. I . . . I started singing. And then the next thing I knew, everything was silent, and I couldn't find Steven. I started swimming back to shore and then I . . . then . . . I found him. Floating face down."

Cole seems to be processing everything in slow motion, his bright hazel eyes turned dark under the waning light of the moon. "You can't hold yourself responsible for that. He *chose* to get into the water at night. I read the police reports myself. It's not your fault."

"But it is, Cole. It is."

He blinks and stops. Glances at the lake. Something shifts in his eyes. A flicker of fear?

"I didn't mean to kill him. I never wanted him to drown. And that's the truth. I didn't know what I was doing when I sang. I didn't know what I was singing at all. But now I know what I am. Know why I wanted to go swimming. I lured him to his death. I'm a siren. It's what I am."

At this, he doesn't move. The moment stretches on and on and on. And then slowly, I see the wheels turning. "I was here a couple of nights ago. I remembering walking here, but then . . . it was like I blacked out. The next thing I knew, I was coughing up lungfuls of water, gasping for breath."

"That was me. I had to . . . drag you out of the lake and give you CPR."

"You saved me?"

"Are you not listening? I drowned you!"

The woods are heavy with silence tonight, no crickets or birds. I just told him everything, and he's just standing there, not even blinking. I wish he'd scream or melt down or run away, because then I'd know what he's thinking. His silence is enough to make me hope, and all hope ever does is hurt me.

"I don't understand. Why would he . . . why would *I* get in the water?"

"It'll be easier to show you." I take in such a huge breath my chest visibly expands. This is it. "Did you bring your iPod?"

He nods and fishes it out of the pocket of his baggy jeans, holding out the tiny red player in the palm of his hand.

I stare at it. It's my fallback plan. If he has those tiny earbuds in his ears, he won't strain against the tree. Won't try desperately to follow me into the lake.

"Put the volume on as high as it goes. Something heavy. Rock or something."

He plays with the dial for a minute, and then music so loud and hard bursts from the headphones I can hear it from where I'm standing, at least four feet away. "Give me your belt."

He raises an eyebrow but does as I ask, sliding it out of the loops. I grip the leather in my hands as I lead him over to the big cedar tree behind us. "Do you trust me?" I ask, searching his dark expression. What if he runs, right now? What if he doesn't even want to know what I'm about to show him?

He nods, swallowing, his hazel eyes wide and genuine, totally unguarded. Even after everything that I've told him, everything that I've done, I can see that he really and truly trusts me, though God knows why.

"Put the headphones in."

He pushes the earbuds into his ears, cringing a little at the volume. He goes to adjust it, but I put my hand on his, shaking my head. He leaves it alone and slips the iPod into the front pocket of his faded jeans.

I take his hands and twist them behind his back. Then I loop his belt tightly around his wrists, over and over until he's shackled to the tree, his arms behind his back. I come around to the front and look into his eyes. They're searching mine for answers. He opens his mouth to speak, but then seems to realize he won't hear my response with the iPod cranked like it is. With no other recourse, he just stands there, his lips parted, a questioning look in his eyes.

This is the moment my life changes.

For better or worse, I have to show him what I am. I want to close my eyes and make some kind of wish, but instead I lean forward and press my lips against his. It may be my last chance to kiss him, and I'm not going to waste it. He leans into me, straining against the pull of the belt. I cup his face in my hands and let the kiss linger for longer than it should.

Then I tear myself away. I step back and unbutton my wet jeans, sliding them down my legs. His eyes glance downward and then flare wide. I don't break eye contact as I slip my sweater over my head.

"Lexi—" he starts, his voice louder than he realizes because the iPod is cranked so loud. His voice seems to echo into the quiet forest.

I put a finger to my lips to silence him, hoping he can't tell how nervous it makes me to know he's watching me as I stand there, nearly naked, but knowing I have no choice. His eyes dart around, as if he expects to catch someone else watching us. Between the way

I'm acting, the darkened sky, and the music blaring in his ears, he must be disoriented, thinking I'm totally crazy.

And maybe I am. My bare feet grow cold against the muddy shore, but for a minute, I can't seem to move away from the intense, confused expression on Cole's face. I've tied him to a tree in the middle of a state forest and here I stand, half-naked.

I step back until I feel the water lap at my toes. And then I stop.

"Can you hear me?"

Cole gives me a confused look. He can't.

Good.

I turn away from him, then take a deep, not-quite-soothing breath and dive in.

I stay under. For a long time. I swim in circles and try to get my hammering heart to slow down. I know that when I come up near the surface, the iridescent glint of my skin will be enough to tell him the truth.

Besides, he has to see how long I can go without air.

Finally, I burst up to the surface, forcing my jaw to clamp down. I need to make sure he still has the iPod on, so I turn to look at him. He's still tied up, still has the earbuds in his ears. He's staring at me, totally, completely still. He could be a statue.

No . . . wait. Something's not right with his expression. It's not shock, or awe, or a thousand things I would expect to see at this point. It's . . . alarm? Is he actually afraid of me? I hadn't expected to see actual fear, real apprehension. . . .

My heart shreds. He's genuinely terrified, by the stark look in his eyes—like I'm going to haul him out and kill him or something.

Our eyes can't seem to tear apart, and I just tread water as I take in the dark fear in his eyes.

And then he moves.

And I realize he's not tied up anymore.

Huh? The shadows shift and rearrange themselves. And then, the full picture seems to focus. It's Erik who takes a step away from the tree. The moonlight falls across his face, casting a weird, grim darkness over his eyes. He gives me a twisted smile, one that sends a chill racing down my spine. He takes another step, toward Cole, toward me.

Fear ripples through me again. Down my spine, settling low in my stomach. There's victory in Erik's look. Like he's won. What is he doing?

And then it gets worse. Sienna steps out from behind another tree, one hand gripping the bark like it's the only thing steadying her.

Pajamas. Somehow that's the first thing I pick up on. She's wearing flannel pants and a dark gray CCH T-shirt, probably something she borrowed from Patrick. I seem to be stuck on the pajamas, staring at them as if they're the most important part of this puzzle. Did Erik go to her house, yank her out of bed, and bring her here?

Panic swells again. How much has she seen? I try to read her expression, and I realize: enough. She's seen enough. I bite hard on the edge of my lip. Hard enough to draw blood.

Why would Erik do this? Why would he ruin everything in one fell swoop?

I throw myself forward, until my bare feet find muddy bank and I climb out of the water. The lake water drips down my hair, slides down my skin. I take a few hurried steps, embarrassed to have an audience when I'm nearly naked. I instinctively go to grab my clothes, but they're missing. Stolen.

I start to step backward, hide my body in the water, but it makes my skin crawl. I don't want to see the iridescent scales on my legs either. I'm not sure what Erik wants, only that he controls the situation. Does he want me in the water, or does he want me out?

And why did he bring Sienna here? To destroy my life completely? Is he panicking because I pushed him away?

I take a few more steps, so that I'm fully on the shore. I should be embarrassed, demand some clothes, but I'm too angry. How could Erik do this? Is he that desperate to separate me from everyone else? Does he think if he isolates me somehow, he'll win?

"What do you think you're doing?" My voice was supposed to be angry, demanding, but it comes out pathetic and shaky.

"Ensuring I get what I deserve." He's standing there as if he owns the lake, his shoulders squared, his smirk cocky.

He looks nothing like the guy I've spent the last few weeks with. *Nothing like him.*

"What the hell does that mean?"

"It means I worked *very* hard to make this all happen, and I'm not going to let you simply throw it away."

"What *are* you?" Sienna bounds forward. Her pink slippers sink into the mud as her hair floats out around her in the breeze left over from the storm. She's inches from me. Her hands ball up and release, flex again, and I brace myself for the punch to the nose I'm sure is coming.

But it doesn't. I blink. Sienna seems to be in shock, not sure what to say to me or why she's saying it. Just that she doesn't understand any of this.

"Did you drive here?" I ask.

She blinks.

I glance over at Erik, who is struggling to keep Cole under control now that he is no longer tied up. I'm not sure how he managed to untie him from the tree and yet still keep his hands bound behind his back. I lower my voice. "Did. You. Drive. Here." Every word is perfectly articulated, low enough that I don't think Erik can hear.

Sienna, bless her soul, nods.

"Leave. Please, if you've ever trusted me a day in your life, leave. And I swear to you, I'll tell you everything tomorrow. Everything. Including the truth about Steven. But you have to go."

Erik knows what I'm doing now, steps forward as if to stop me, his smirk turned into a frown. He didn't count on this. On Sienna listening to me for a second, once she saw who I was. On Sienna actually having a mind of her own.

I stare into her eyes for a long moment. They look so much like Steven's, it's hard not to look away as the pain snakes around my heart. And then . . . she spins around. Runs. Her blonde hair streams behind her as she leaps over a log, breaks into a sprint as the sticks in her path snap under her weight.

A tiny piece of me relaxes. And then I turn to Erik, surprised that he let her go. "You need to leave. This isn't right and you know it. You'll never get what you want this way."

"You don't even know what I want." He looks pleased, which sends a shiver of fear down my spine. There's such a weird gleam of satisfaction in his eyes, like the cat that has the canary.

I grit my teeth. "This isn't something you can force me into. You want me to give you forever, and I can't even give you a day. It'll never work. Just let me go. Let *him* go."

He just laughs. "You don't get it, do you? I don't want forever. I never did," he says, giving Cole a little shove. "I was *never* going to fall in love with you. Yes, love can break your curse, but I don't give a damn about your bloody curse."

He pauses, takes in my expression, and grins wider. "See, I'm not cursed to be a nix. Unless you think a horse is cursed to be a horse. I *am* a nix. Forever and always, a creature of the river. It's not so bad, really. I get to control people. Drown them when I feel like it." That creepy smile envelops his face. "And I *feel like it* fairly often."

Cole's eyes flare wider. He's just realized he's in danger. That Erik is capable of more than either of us ever realized. He starts to take a step away from Erik, toward me, but Erik is too fast for him. He grabs the back of Cole's shirt and yanks him.

I'm frozen, blindsided by the harsh reality of who Erik is, by the fact that I stupidly trusted everything he told me. I was too desperate for it all to be true.

"Is *anything* you said true? Is your mom even a siren?"

The smirk returns as he shakes his head, and then it grows into an ugly, arrogant smile, as if he just came into possession of the world and is about to wave it in front of me before yanking it away. He reaches out and shoves Cole so abruptly that Cole falls to his knees. Because he's still shackled, he doesn't put his hands out to catch himself, just falls facedown.

I step forward again, shivering from fear, not quite sure if I should leap forward and launch myself at Erik, or if there's some more logical way out of this.

Erik turns his attention from Cole to me. Something foreign glitters in his eyes. "You were easier than the other sirens. The guilt of killing made you desperate to believe there was a way out. All I had to do was paint a pretty picture, and you were mine."

I don't blink, don't move. Every muscle in my body seems to go slack at once, as if my entire body wants to give out. I stare at him, the lake water still lapping at my ankles. His devilish smirk grows until he looks possessed.

"At this point, you're supposed to ask *why*. Why you. Why a siren." He pauses. "It's because humans are so easy to kill. A pretty face like mine, and they fall for anything. They practically walk into the river, and all I have to do is smile. You've killed one, you've killed a thousand. And in four hundred years, I've killed at least that many."

Four hundred years.

He told me he was turning eighteen.

And that's when it occurs to me: It was never his ancestors who scorned the disfigured women. It was him. All along, it was him. He didn't inherit his curse. He was *personally* cursed. He's a sociopath. A complete and utter sociopath.

"Do you remember Kate?"

I swallow. Do I play his game? Keep this conversation going? "The girl you told me about at homecoming? The one you fell in love with?"

He nods. "I stumbled upon her one night, a hundred and fifty years ago."

The story he told me. About a nix finding a siren . . . It was Erik and Kate, not two strangers a century and a half ago.

"My favorite river fed into the ocean where she swam." He pauses. "She was beautiful. I fell in love with her within the month."

I wait for the punch line I am sure is coming.

"But she didn't love me. I broke her curse, and still she didn't love me." He looks off into the distance. "So I drowned her."

My horror grows, along with the smile on his face. "And then I went back to the status quo. Drowning women in the river. The only thing that ever gave me satisfaction.

"But I got bored after a while, and then I got an idea. I find another siren, bring her to the water *before* her curse is broken . . . well, she'll put up a real struggle. Sirens can hold their breath so much longer, it makes the whole fight more challenging. And I do enjoy a challenge."

I step forward, hope he forgets Cole is standing in front of him. "What the hell was the point of all this then? Why feed me all these lies? Why get to know me? I've been to this lake every night. You could have killed me by now."

To this, his grin widens. "You ever watch a cat kill a mouse? They don't just go for the lethal blow. Not when it's so much more fun to play with a victim. Killing *is* a sort of seduction, you know."

"You're disgusting."

"Ah, and yet you nearly fell for me. Pity this all ends so soon. I would have *so* enjoyed hearing those three words before I drowned you." He smirks. "You're the eighth, you know. The number would be higher, except it takes so long to find your kind. You're just not as common as one might think."

He screws his mouth up to the side as if deep in thought, but it's all part of his theatricalities. "The last one fell for me in thirty-nine days. I only gave myself three weeks with you, once I was sure you were a siren. Perhaps that was too greedy of me."

It's as if my toes have turned into roots and grown right into the bank of the lake. I can't seem to move, not even an inch. I can't believe I was so blindsided.

He frowns. "Which leads me to this," he says, his hand sweeping across the lake. "Your time is up. And lucky for you, so is his. So you can have him after all, *as long as you both shall live.*" He says the last part as if it's a marriage vow.

He reaches out and kicks Cole, sending him facedown into the mud. I jump forward to help, but Erik puts a hand up, and the look in his eyes is enough to stop me. Cole wriggles around, trying to get to his knees again, but his arms are bound so tightly he can't get up. Erik seems to enjoy watching him squirm. "Don't get me wrong, you've been fun at times. But you're a little on the boring side. Too studious, too serious. The last siren, well, she was a partier. Drowned her sorrows, if you know what I mean."

Erik waves both hands around maniacally, as the panic rises in my stomach. He's hanging by a thread now, and I don't have any plan for getting out of this mess. I turn to look at Cole again, desperation growing. This wasn't supposed to happen. This isn't why I brought him here. If only I'd known . . . "Just let him go, Erik. This is between me and you."

Erik leans down and hauls Cole to his feet. Erik has at least three or four inches, not to mention twenty or thirty pounds, on Cole. If they go at it, Cole's a dead man. That ugly, devilish smirk rises on Erik's lips, and he takes a step away from me.

"See, that's where you're wrong. It *is* about Cole. This guy is so in love with you, he'll probably love you in spite of all this, and then your curse is gone. So he's gotta go, while you're still a siren and still fun for me. I need you to be cursed, or haven't you figured that out yet?"

Erik takes another step. Toward the lake.

"Stop," I say, my voice as steady as I can manage. "This is stupid! You can't just—"

And then he half throws, half shoves Cole, who flies into the water, headfirst. The water isn't very deep that close to shore, but with his hands behind his back . . .

I scramble across the bank and throw myself into the water. I'm stopped when, midway between the land and the lake, I collide with Erik. His arms lock around me. The momentum sends the two of us back into the water.

And then something's not right. We're moving backward, almost floating, but I don't feel Erik taking steps as he drags me into the water. I blink and look down, at where my legs meet the surface, and my heart jumps straight into my throat.

I never asked . . . never wondered what he looked like in the water. I assumed he'd look like me, with shimmery blue skin. But . . . it's not like that at all. His legs have disappeared, replaced with scaled limbs. More like something on a dragon, a deep red.

His favorite color is red.

Except, they're not like legs, either. They're . . . like tentacles, long, winding, slithering around underneath the surface like a den of snakes. I get my hands up and put them against his chest, and then shove hard, and thanks to the water his grip loosens. I slide out. The second I have enough gap, I drop down, under the water, out of his grasp, and throw myself into a swim.

Cole could be underwater right now. Struggling for air . . . his lungs filling with the lake. . . .

My head breaks through the surface, and I take in a ragged breath as the water trails rivers down my face, in my eyes. I blink several times, and with relief, I see Cole.

Just as I think I'm going to make it to shore—to where Cole is coughing and sputtering, wriggling out of the lake because his hands are still tied behind his back, Erik gets a hold of my ankle. I slide backward, under the surface and into the deeper area of the lake. I take a gasp of air a second before I go under.

I will my heart to slow, try to get the panic to ebb so that my oxygen will last longer, but all I can do is blink against the water. Red tentacles flare out all around me. Erik drags me deeper. This must be what it's like when he finds a girl and drags her into the river.

This must be exactly what it's like. He's going to drown me.

I twist, struggling against his hold. But it does nothing. I claw at the bottom of the lake, trying to find something strong enough to hold on to, trying to keep him from dragging me deeper. My fingernails claw at the muddy bottom but come up empty.

This lake isn't that big. But it's big enough to drown in. My fingers slide across something, but it goes by so quickly I can't figure out what it is. With a sudden burst of energy, I drag Erik back—just a foot—far enough that I find it again before he drags me even deeper.

A stick. A little thinner and a little longer than a baseball bat, by the feel of it. It's getting hard to see with all the silt and dirt we're stirring up. I grip it in two hands and then twist around and throw everything I have into swinging it, right at his face, and those glowing blue eyes that only just register what's about to happen.

The water slows it down, but I still manage to crack him hard enough that his grip loosens. I hurtle myself forward, swimming faster than I ever have. When I get shallow enough, I surface, raking in big lungfuls of air.

Cole has somehow gotten the belt off and is stepping into the lake, as if he's going to help me. As if he wouldn't drown before he even understood what was happening. "Go! Run!"

My feet find the bottom, and I rush from the lake. If we can get away from the water, our odds are better. But in the water, we don't stand a chance.

Cole hesitates. Just a millisecond, he wavers, before whirling and running, crashing straight into a bush and falling back down. My bare feet slip on the mud, and then I yank him back to his feet and shove him toward the trail. He takes off running, the underbrush cracking as he races by.

That's the last thing I see before Erik's hand clamps over my eyes and mouth, and I feel myself falling backward, into the water. I can't take another gasp of air before going under, because Erik is blocking my nose and mouth.

Erik holds me against his body in an iron grip, my arms trapped at my sides. I struggle against him, but his grip is too strong. He spins around a few times underwater, like a washing machine, until I don't even know which way is up.

The breath I took before he covered my mouth is not enough. My lungs already burn. I'm going to drown.

Erik stops spinning, but doesn't let go. He squeezes tighter, as if he's going to crush the life right out of me. Black holes crop up in my vision. I can't let him do this. I can't die like this. I struggle harder, using the last of my strength. But it's no use.

I'm really going to die, right here in the lake that's helped me live all this time.

And then something in the mud-churned water takes focus. Eyes. Hazel ones. Cole's face looms closer, as if he's going to kiss me. And then his lips . . .

Am I imagining this? Dreaming of Cole in my last moment?

No, no, he's not kissing me, he's . . . *breathing* for me. I take in the air he's giving me, and the black holes ebb, and my strength returns. I jerk abruptly, elbowing Erik, and the shock in my attack is enough to jar his focus. His grip slips.

I yank free and grab Cole's arm, pushing him in front of me. With my help he makes it out of the lake before Erik can get a hold of him. We fall onto the shore, and just as I take a ragged, deep breath of air, I hear Erik coming for me.

For us.

I whirl around, desperate for relief, and I see something. The one thing that could end this. Just as Erik drags me backward again, I slap my hand down on Cole's belt. It nearly slips through my fingers, but then Cole manages to snag the buckle and flip it in my direction, and my fingers curl around the buttery leather.

I take in another breath, the biggest I can manage, as he pulls me under. Before he can wrap his arms around me, I twist, somehow managing to get behind him. He tries to turn and face me, but I wrap my legs around his waist. He's so bulky they almost don't hook on the other side, but all I can do is pray he doesn't thrash too hard until I can get the belt around Erik's neck.

As soon as the leather touches his skin, he knows. And he jerks and twists and outmuscles me, but somehow I just squeeze tighter with my legs and get the belt fed through the buckle.

Erik realizes what I'm doing and turns his attention to my legs, gripping each ankle painfully in one of his big hands. I think he could crush my bones with his grip. I ignore the pierce of pain as he untangles my legs from his waist. It's too late for him.

I tighten the belt around Erik's neck. I use both hands to hold the end, until I'm sure it's as tight as it can go. And then I switch into offensive mode, hoping I have enough strength to do what comes next.

Erik thrashes like a prized bronco, but I manage to get my legs around his waist again when his focus is on the belt. I squeeze as hard as possible, then close my eyes and wait.

Wait to see who will die.

It goes on forever, or so it seems, my limbs trembling with the effort. Erik seems as strong as ever, thrashing, spinning, scraping me against the bottom of the lake. Whenever my head surfaces, I take in great gasping breaths, then tighten down on the belt again.

Twice, he plunges as deeply as possible, his body slamming me into the muddy bottom. I nearly open my mouth and let out the air that he's trying to force from my lungs.

But I just keep holding on.

And then something changes. His struggles grow weaker, about the time my own air seems to be running out. But still I don't let go. I open my eyes when he goes still, watch the eerie way his platinum hair floats out in front of me. My bare toes find the lake bottom, and I walk backward, dragging him, until finally my head breaks through the surface. I take a ragged breath, filling my screaming, aching lungs.

Water splashes around me as Cole grabs me by the waist and pulls me backward, still dragging Erik's heavy body.

I don't let him go until I'm out of the water and the three of us all fall backward. For a long silent moment, all we can do is rake in one heavy breath after another. My wet back presses against Cole's chest, his ragged breathing matching mine.

But finally, I shift out of his embrace, pull my legs out from underneath Erik's now still body, and let go of the belt still gripped in my aching fingers.

I'm afraid to look at him, but I have to know.

I crawl closer to Erik. His lips are blue, his skin clammy and white, unnatural. Although I want anything but to be close to him, I lean in, listen for him to take a breath, then feel for a pulse.

He's really dead. I've really killed him.

I rock back on my heels and stare, unmoving, for much too long. Waiting for signs of life, waiting for answers as to what I should do now. But he doesn't move.

"You had to do it," Cole says. "He would have killed you. And me. Probably, Sienna."

I swallow and nod, finally tearing my eyes away from Erik.

Rain begins to fall around us again, waking me. Water drips down Cole's dark curls into his eyes. "What do we do with him now?"

Do with him? He's dead. I glance over at him. At the large body sitting in the mud.

Oh. He means the body.

"I—" I start to speak, but I don't know what I was going to say. What is there to say, really?

My eyes swim out of focus for a minute. "There's a river right past that tree line." I pause, the irony of sending Erik to the river isn't lost on me. I continue, regardless. "It's wide and deep. We can drag him over there, toss him in. It'll carry him all the way to the ocean."

Neither of us moves for a minute. "They'll know he was strangled."

"They'd never think it's me. I'm half his size. They'll have no evidence, no crime scene. How can they even identify him? He's four hundred years old. Maybe he forged some records, but if they dig into it . . . it won't hold up."

Cole just sits there for a long minute. "Okay, let's do it."

But neither of us gets up. Instead, we just sit there on the muddy shore as the rain grows heavier. We're both already soaked anyway.

"How long have you been . . .?"

"A siren?"

He nods.

"I always felt drawn to the ocean, but the real pull didn't start until my sixteenth birthday. The night—" I stop. "The night I swam with Steven."

"Is he the only . . .?"

"Yes. Until tonight anyway. That's why I call this lake *mine*. It's the only way I can avoid killing anyone. I have to swim every night or I get sick, and I need somewhere no one can hear me sing. If someone hears me . . . they'll walk right into the water."

"Had to," he says.

"What?"

"Past tense. Had to."

I blink and stare at him, a lump growing in my throat. "What are you saying?"

"I don't give a damn about all this. It might be what you are, but it's not *who* you are."

My mouth goes dry. "I killed someone. I killed *two* people. You need to think about this. Really process it and realize what you're saying—"

"I know what I'm saying. And I love you."

A tear trails down my cheek. Three words I thought I'd never hear from him.

It won't take long to find out if they're real.

CHAPTER THIRTY-TWO

On the way back to Cole's house, I turn into Sienna's driveway. Her house, pitch-black, stretches out in front of me. Her parents must be gone again. It seems like they're always gone these days. I guess in some ways, Sienna is more alone than I am. I try to remember the last time I saw her parents, or even heard her mention them, but I can't.

I hope she's okay right now, in that big dark house.

I turn and look at Cole. "Can you . . . can you wait out here? I think I need to do this on my own. I owe her that much."

He nods and kisses me on the forehead, then gives my hand a squeeze. "Good luck."

I take in a big gulp of air. "Thanks. I'll need it."

I climb out of my car, leaving it running with the heat cranked. Cole's hair is still wet, matted to his forehead, and we're both exhausted. But it didn't seem right to go home without seeing Sienna, making sure she made it back okay.

I walk to the front door, pausing for a second to glance back at Cole, hoping for a reassuring smile, but it's hard to see more than his shadow behind the glass. I turn back to the front door and knock, fidgeting as I stand there.

Nothing.

I knock again, glancing back at my car. Still, no answer. I step down off the porch and walk around the other side of the house, peering into the dark windows. She must be home by now. Where else would she go?

I knock on the backdoor, but again, no one answers. Reluctantly, I turn the knob, surprised when it clicks open. The soft melody of pop music floats from Sienna's bedroom. Maybe she didn't hear me knocking.

I push the door shut, then turn around in the darkness and call out to her. "Sienna?"

Nothing. The hairs on the back of my neck prickle. I walk slowly, cautiously, across the kitchen, toward her room. "Hello?"

I knock softly on the door, and it nudges open. Warning bells go off in my head. The room is shadowed, quiet except for the music. I almost don't see her.

She's sitting on the window seat, staring out at the closed drapes, still as a statue. Shadows stretch along the corners of the room, creep up around me. Why is she sitting in the dark? Staring at nothing?

I swallow. "Sienna?"

She turns and looks at me. Her hair is disheveled, her eyes red-rimmed. She hasn't changed since she left the lake, mud still clinging to the hem of her pajama pants.

"You killed him, didn't you?" Her voice is cold, icy, devoid of all emotion, except an undercurrent of anger.

My mouth goes dry.

"Who?" *Please say Erik.*

"Steven. Erik came over, said there was something really important for me to see, and I followed him up those godforsaken gravel roads for miles. He refused to say a word until we got to the lake, and then he couldn't stop talking. He called you a siren. Told me that I could hear your voice, but Cole couldn't, or you'd drown him. He was disappointed when you didn't sing right away. He was going to pull Cole's headphones off and let him walk into the water."

A wave of horror overpowers me. Erik was never going to be the one to kill Cole.

I was.

She turns just enough to let her legs dangle off the edge of the window seat. She's so short they don't reach the floor. "I can't stop thinking about it. About the way you've acted these last two years. It wasn't an accident. You killed Steven. *You* are the reason he walked into the ocean."

My heart beats louder in my ears.

Sienna's voice is razor thin, barely controlled. She's glaring at me, waiting for an answer.

My breath comes harder, faster, and I fight to choke the tears down. "Sienna, you don't understand. It *was* an accident. I didn't mean to. I didn't even know what I was doing—"

Sienna whips around, grabs the glass of water, and hurls it at me. I duck just in time—it whistles right past my head before shattering against her bedroom wall. I stay crouched on the floor for a heart-thumping moment, and then shakily get to my feet to see the anger blazing in her eyes.

The secret that had been wedged between us all this time has now ripped us apart.

"You *had* to know how much it ate at me, not knowing why he drowned," she screams. "He was a good swimmer, and I knew the police were wrong. *You had to know* how hard it's been to let him go when none of it made sense!"

She grits her teeth so hard I'm shocked they don't break.

"I don't want to talk to you," she says, her voice turning low, boiling with fury. "I don't want to *see* you. You will change classes. You will stay away from my family, my friends, my fucking lunch table. If you *ever* speak to me again, I will expose you for what you are."

"Sien—"

"Go. Now." She picks up something else from the table next to her—it looks like small jewelry box—and I scramble backward and knock her bedroom door open so hard it punches a small indent in her drywall.

I run through the house, nearly tripping on an area rug, and throw open the front door. My throat hurts—burns with unshed tears. I shove the door shut and struggle to get my feet to work properly.

Cole gets out of the car and rushes to me. I fall into him.

Everything Sienna and I shared, everything we tried to get back, it's over. I'll never have my best friend back. It hurts even more than

I could have imagined. Hurts more than when I lost her the first time. Because now I know what it's like without her, and I don't want to go back to that. But she knows the truth now. She knows I murdered her brother. And she'll never let me in again.

Cole takes in my wild look, and his eyes dart over to her house. "She didn't—"

"No." I gulp back the tears. "She's not . . . She hates me."

"I'm sorry," he says, going to hug me.

I pull away. "Let's just get out of here, okay? Let's just go to your house."

I glance back at Sienna's house one more time as I climb into the car, wondering if I'll ever set foot in it again, knowing I won't.

Friendship only survives so much.

I take a shower in Cole's bathroom, relishing the sting of the hot water over my skin. Every part of me aches, and there are bluish spots all over my body from the fight with Erik. If I could, I'd spend all night in the hot steam of the shower.

I wince as I rub a bar of soap over my sore ribs. It's like someone put me inside a dryer and left me there for an hour, tumbling around in the barrel. I switch the water off, towel dry, and pull the T-shirt and boxers Cole loaned me and over my limbs. I run a comb through my hair, watching the gentle waves spring back to life.

Not even a murder attempt is enough to ruin my hair.

I stare at myself in the mirror, try to recognize myself. So many things changed tonight.

For starters, I killed again. When Erik told me he loved me, part of me realized I had to leave him. But I never planned on killing him. I grip the edge of the countertop and close my eyes, unable to look back at myself any longer

It doesn't matter that it was self-defense. That Erik would have surely killed me if I hadn't done it. I still ended another life. I swallow, willing the tears away. I don't want to kill again. *Ever* again. I've lost so much because of the water. And now that Erik is gone, now that I know he could never really solve my curse, I might be right back where I started.

If Erik was really lying . . . if this goes on forever . . . I don't know how long I can handle it. Handle what I am.

A knock on the door makes me jump. "You okay?"

I nod, then realize he can't see me. "Yep," I say, forcing my voice to remain neutral.

"Then can you come out of there and talk to me?"

I sigh. Then I double-check that my eyes aren't as red-rimmed as they feel, and I leave the quiet of his bathroom.

When I walk into his bedroom, my bare feet padding across the luxurious carpet, the nerves in my stomach multiply. Cole sits at the edge of his bed, a remote in his hand, the blue of the television basking him in an odd glow. He's wearing a faded gray T-shirt, his dark wet hair gracing the collar. He looks natural, at ease in his own environment.

I stop at the foot of the bed and swallow, fighting the urge to wring my hands. I know he must have more questions, but I don't know if he's going to like the answers.

There has to be a moment he steps back and realizes this isn't worth it. That *I'm* not worth it.

He flicks off the television and drops the remote. The only light in the room comes from the porch light outside, an odd yellow light between the cracks of the partially closed curtains. Cole stands and steps toward me, slinging his arms around my shoulders and crushing me against him.

Relief floods through me as I rest my cheek against his shoulder, breathing in the fresh scent of his bar soap, the same scent that still lingers on my skin. His body is warm, soft, secure, and I could stand like this all day, ignoring the pain on my skin and in my heart.

He steps back just a bit and tilts my head upward with one finger. My eyes snap shut as his lips crash into mine. In a mass of kisses and limbs, we tumble back onto his bed.

Something's different this time. The wall Cole put up whenever we used do this . . . whenever we went this far . . . is somewhere left behind. We're twisting and grabbing, pieces of clothing dropping to the floor. His lips are everywhere, my hands sliding up and down his body.

We can't get enough. Is it a near-death experience, driving us to act like this? Our breaths come in loud, heavy rasps. Cole moves to his nightstand to reach for something, and I nearly yank him back to me. But then he's back and settling on top of me; and when finally, there's nothing between us, his entire body against mine, hot skin on skin, our eyes lock.

"I love you," I whisper, my fingers raking across his bare back. I hadn't planned to say it, but the words float out with a sigh.

He leans down, rests his forehead against mine so that our eyes are so close, all I can see is a mass of brown and green swirling together, intense with emotion and need. "I love you, too."

I shut my eyes to keep the lone tear from escaping.

For the first time in my life, I'm not lonely.

• • •

I jolt awake.

Awake.

I gasp and spring upright so fast and clumsy that I twist and fall out of bed, yanking the blanket with me in one big puddle of limbs and sheets.

My breath and heart race so fast they compete, and I can't hear anything but the freight train in my ears. I blink over and over, trying to see in the darkness.

Cole is at my side in an instant, hauling me to my feet. "What's wrong? What happened?"

My voice comes out so quiet, so low, it's barely enough to call it a whisper. "I slept."

"What?"

"I slept," I say, louder this time, though still shaky. Cole guides me back to the bed, and I sit, perched, on the edge of it. I glance at the clock on his nightstand.

It's three forty. I slept over three hours. I wiggle my shoulders, flap my arms around, swing my feet off the edge of the bed. I feel . . . better. Some of the achiness has gone away. The sandy feeling behind my eyelids seems to have dissipated. The weight on my shoulders feels like someone removed a few bricks.

"I slept!" I say, louder now, throwing my arms around him. Heat warms my face. We're both still naked.

I twist around, start scooping clothes off the floor before my cheeks burst into flames. I've never been naked in front of a boy before, not like this.

Cole tosses me my shirt and then pulls on his own. "And this is newsworthy?" He's confused but relieved, too, as he realizes nothing is wrong.

I yank my borrowed boxers up over my hips. "Yes! You don't understand, Cole. Normal people sleep. People who don't have curses. I *do not* sleep, at least not for the last two years. I swim. I go up to the lake."

He blinks rapidly. Understanding dawns. "So . . . he wasn't lying? You don't have to swim now?"

"I don't know! I think so?" I sit down on the edge of his bed, deflated a little. "I did swim last night, a little. Maybe that's all this is. But then . . . that really doesn't explain why I slept. Just why I didn't need to swim."

What if this is meaningless? What if I'm just worn out from fighting off Erik all night, and this is just . . . temporary? A heavy silence falls around us. We stare at the ground, sitting side by side on his bed, neither of us speaking.

Hope builds. It might actually be possible. What if this whole time all I needed was to fall in love? With someone who knew the truth and somehow... loved me anyway?

Maybe that's why Erik went after Cole first. He wanted me to kill him. Make sure I never got what I wanted.

"It can't be this simple," I say, more to myself than to Cole. "It can't possibly be this simple."

Cole grips my hand. "Occam's Razor."

"What?"

He turns to look at me. "It's usually the simplest answer that's the right one."

Nervous, I stand up abruptly and walk to the window, pushing the curtain open. The moon gleams over the ocean, the waves rolling gently to shore. I stare at it for a long moment in silence, waiting to feel that familiar hunger, the strong pull of the ocean. But I feel nothing.

I twist around. "You really think it was you, all along? That trusting you . . . falling for you . . . was the one thing that could undo this whole mess?"

I want to laugh and cry all at once. If it's true. . . everything with Erik was for nothing.

Cole stands, shrugging as he walks up to me, pushes a stray, tangled strand of hair over my shoulder. "I don't know . . . but . . . it could be, right?"

I swallow and nod.

Yes, it's possible.

Yes, it seems too good to be true.

"We need to go outside. I need to stand on the beach. But if I make one move, if I so much as dip my toes in the surf, you plug your ears and run the other way. No matter what I do. Got it?"

"Yeah. Let me get dressed." He pulls his pajama pants back on and goes to the closet, taking a hoodie off the top shelf. Then he tosses one at me, and I'm so deep in thought I barely manage to catch it.

He holds the door open for me as I slip into the sweatshirt, my arms lost inside the sleeves. It's warm and soft and smells like the woodsy scent I've missed these last few weeks. He told me he liked going to Tillamook Forest. It must be why he always smelled like the woods.

Cole steps up beside me and reaches for my hand. I surprise

myself by pulling away. "Can you just . . . stay, like, thirty feet away? I'm afraid if we're touching and I want the ocean, I'll drag you in."

He furrows his brow. "Lexi, you'd never—"

"I don't trust myself. And right now, you shouldn't either. Just do it."

Cole sighs and steps away from me, trailing a dozen yards behind as we reach the beach. My shoes sink as I make my way across, until I'm standing at the edge of the moist, compact sand, just a few feet shy of the line of foam left behind by the waves.

Cole stops where he is, watching me.

I turn to the ocean and stare outward, waiting. Nothing happens. I peer down and push the button on the side of my watch, illuminating the display. 3:57. I should want to swim right now. I should *need* to swim right now, in the darkness of night, standing on the beach in the middle of the night.

But it's like waiting on the tracks for a train that never comes. Nothing happens.

I glance back at him again, and then out at the sea.

And then before I know what's happening, I'm crying, and Cole is standing beside me, pulling me close.

Moments later, when he tips my chin up, I don't resist.

I just kiss him.

CHAPTER THIRTY-THREE

A week later, I step through the gates of Seaside Cemetery, my sneakers crunching on the leaves that line the paths. I pull Cole's sweater tighter around me as a sharp October breeze bites through. It's a brisk, chilly walk to Steven's grave, a walk I've made so many times before. But this time is different.

This time I'm not alone.

We navigate between the headstones, the world silent around us except for the sound of our shoes on the frosty grass. We make our way to the stone with the football engraved in the middle, a meticulous piece of solid-white perfectly polished granite. It will last forever, so much longer than Steven.

We stop in front of it, and Cole puts an arm around my waist. I lean into him, and we stand in silence as I purse my lips and stare at the stone for a long time, my eyes staring at the dates, at the year I killed him.

He's been resting in the earth for two years. Two years the world has gone without that goofy, crooked smile, without his jokes. It still aches to think about him, to picture the light in his eyes and know that I'm the one who extinguished it.

Sienna will never be my friend again. I had to beg and plead, but I was able to transfer out of her English class. Cole and I eat lunch in the library now, reading books and whispering. I feel bad for taking him away from his friends, but he understands. He knows I don't want it like this, but there's nothing I can do to change it. So he chooses me over them.

Steven will never come back. What I did to him . . . I can't undo. Their whole family is broken because of me.

But somehow, I have to find a way to move on. With Cole, it's actually possible. I don't have to swim anymore. I haven't since that night at the lake with Erik. As psychotic as he was, it seems that not everything he said was a lie.

Cole really did break my curse.

With each sunset, it gets easier to believe that the curse is really broken, easier to look forward instead of back. I'll do things just as I always said—go to college, find a way to give back to the world the things I took.

I step forward, brush my fingers against the top of the grave marker. I'm not sure I can meet Cole's eyes. "Talking to Steven is the only thing that kept me sane these couple of years." I chew on my lip. "Which is kind of ridiculous, since killing him is what broke me in the first place."

"It's not ridiculous." Silence. And then, "You know it's not your fault, right? You're not a murderer. You didn't know what you were doing."

I blink. I know that, even though sometimes I question it. I always will. Yet hearing Cole say it aloud is comforting.

"You okay?" he asks.

I turn to face him, smiling a little. I wonder if he'll ever stop asking me that. "Yeah. Can you give me a second?"

Cole nods, steps away, and goes to stand under the weeping willow. It's bare now, what's left of its thin leaves littering the lawn between the graves.

I crouch in front of the grave. There's nothing left to say to him, because I've already told him everything I can. I've apologized, I've cried, I've made promises. I've told him every secret, every ache. He's been there for me in a way no one else could be.

But the words don't matter anymore.

It's time to move on.

I exhale a ragged breath of air as I stand, pressing my fingers to my lips, and then brush them against the cold marble of his grave.

"*Good-bye, Steven.*"

This time, I mean it.

ACKNOWLEDGMENTS

Every time I write an acknowledgments page, it's different. But there is one constant: My agent Zoe, who is my fiercest advocate, and the one who keeps me from going crazy during the process of making a book. Thank you for all that you do—and for not slapping me with a dead fish by now.

I must also sincerely thank my editor, Jocelyn. This book was acquired before you joined Razorbill, and I was terrified you wouldn't have the same passion for Lexi and her story, but my worries were unwarranted. I cannot even imagine what this book would look like if it weren't for your input. You kicked my butt, and for that, I thank you. My sincerest, gratitude, also, to Gillian for your input during edits.

Thank you, as well, to Ben, who wanted nothing to do with "a mermaid book," but gave *Ripple* a chance anyway.

For Billy, Sammy, and Bridget, thank you for coming through at a moment's notice and pointing out where the story jumped the shark.

And Cyn, as always, I appreciate your honesty—and your ability to be blunt as hell. My career is better because I know you.

My love to my husband, who left the house time and again with our daughter just to give me time to write; this book would have come out sometime in 2035 if it weren't for you. Your love and support mean the world to me.

Finally, thank you to my readers, who cared enough to email me about *Prada And Prejudice* or *You Wish*. Your emails never fail to make my day.